STEPPING INTO THE MIDDLE OF HELL

Don't exactly know where the first shot came from. Way I stood in the street made it hard to see most of them boys. But it sounded like someone from the Pitt bunch fired the round that tipped us all into a bloody inferno. Could have been someone from either camp, though, I suppose.

Truth is, the concussion from that first blast almost blew my hat off. Marshal Stonehill went down like a burlap bag of horseshoes. Every hair on the back of my neck turned into barbed wire.

Nick Fox went for his guns. We were so close to one another, the highly concentrated wad of a double fistful of lead damn near blew him in half. Dropped both hammers of the shotgun on his sorry ass. Splattered him all over the board fence. Pistols popped out of holsters all over the street like rabbits from a traveling magician's hat.

I headed for the doorway of the barbershop fast as I could hoof it. Arrived just in time to turn and watch as men from the Tingwell gang pushed their way into the Matador, while wildly firing over their shoulders. Front window of that cow-country oasis exploded in a hailstorm of shattered glass.

BAD BLOOD

LUCIUS DODGE AND THE
REDLANDS WAR

J. LEE BUTTS

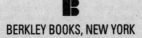
BERKLEY BOOKS, NEW YORK

THE BERKLEY PUBLISHING GROUP
Published by the Penguin Group
Penguin Group (USA) Inc.
375 Hudson Street, New York, New York 10014, USA
Penguin Group (Canada), 90 Eglinton Avenue East, Suite 700, Toronto, Ontario M4P 2Y3, Canada
(a division of Pearson Penguin Canada Inc.)
Penguin Books Ltd., 80 Strand, London WC2R 0RL, England
Penguin Group Ireland, 25 St. Stephen's Green, Dublin 2, Ireland (a division of Penguin Books Ltd.)
Penguin Group (Australia), 250 Camberwell Road, Camberwell, Victoria 3124, Australia
(a division of Pearson Australia Group Pty. Ltd.)
Penguin Books India Pvt. Ltd., 11 Community Centre, Panchsheel Park, New Delhi—110 017, India
Penguin Group (NZ), Cnr. Airborne and Rosedale Roads, Albany, Auckland 1310, New Zealand
(a division of Pearson New Zealand Ltd.)
Penguin Books (South Africa) (Pty.) Ltd., 24 Sturdee Avenue, Rosebank, Johannesburg 2196,
South Africa

Penguin Books Ltd., Registered Offices: 80 Strand, London WC2R 0RL, England

This is a work of fiction. Names, characters, places, and incidents either are the product of the author's imagination or are used fictitiously, and any resemblance to actual persons, living or dead, business establishments, events, or locales is entirely coincidental.

BAD BLOOD

A Berkley Book / published by arrangement with the author

PRINTING HISTORY
Berkley edition / August 2005

ISBN: 0-425-20352-2

BERKLEY®
Berkley Books are published by The Berkley Publishing Group,
a division of Penguin Group (USA) Inc.,
375 Hudson Street, New York, New York 10014.
BERKLEY is a registered trademark of Penguin Group (USA) Inc.
The "B" design is a trademark belonging to Penguin Group (USA) Inc.

PRINTED IN THE UNITED STATES OF AMERICA

10 9 8 7 6 5 4 3 2 1

ACKNOWLEDGMENTS

Special thanks to Kimberly Lionetti for her continued faith, belief, help, and understanding. Much gratitude to Samantha Mandor for all her efforts on my behalf. Texas longhorn kudos to the DFW Writers' Workshop—the absolute best place in the country for an aspiring writer to hone his craft.

"Damn all family feuds and inherited scraps," muttered Ranse *vindictively to the breeze as he rode back to the Cibolo.*

—O. Henry, *The Higher Abdication*

"The fault, dear Brutus, is not in our stars, but in ourselves . . ."

—*Julius Caesar* I, ii, 134

"Whoso sheddeth man's blood, by man shall his blood be shed: for in the image of God made he man."

—Genesis 9:6

1

"PUT ENOUGH BUCKSHOT IN HIS BACK TO MAKE A BOAT ANCHOR"

'FORE GOD I swear ain't nothing like the rigors of advanced age for setting a man's mind to wandering. Seems like everything I see these days reminds me of something, or someone, from my explosive past.

Visited Cooley Churchpew's place yesterday. He runs a grocery and mercantile outfit about five miles up a dirt road from my Sulphur River ranch. Yanked open his screen door, the one with a rusted Nehi Cola sign dangling from a single screw, and almost stomped all over a young woman on her way out. Damned good-looking gal. Had red hair, blue eyes, and smelled like chubby little angels had bathed her in something wild and expensive. Thought for a minute I'd seen the ghost of Ruby Black. Sent shivers all the way to the soles of my muddy boots.

Finished my business with Cooley quick as I could. Jumped back in Ezemerelda, my should-be-in-the-scrap-heap pickup truck, and headed home all flusterated and shaky. Flopped into my favorite back-porch chair, rolled a smoke, and poured myself an extra large tumbler of bonded Kentucky bourbon. Spent the next hour or so watching the sun sink to the bottom of the river.

Something about the way light bounced off the sparkling water, and that little gal's fiery hair, transported me back more'n sixty years—a summer of matchless heat, windblown gun smoke, and uninvited death. The past has such power, you know. It can jump up and gobsmack you right into another time and place as easy as eatin' fried chicken with your fingers.

Summer of 1879, or maybe '80, I think, but don't hold me to it as the righteous truth. Not certain of the year but, by God, I remember the weather—hotter than a fresh-forged horseshoe. Camp dogs had taken almost every bit of shade available. Lack of water caused cottonwoods to shed their leaves so fast that standing under one was similar to being in a snowstorm. Live oaks drooped like creek-dwelling willows. Light breeze didn't do much of anything toward relief. Simply carried a gritty layer of Texas topsoil into every exposed wrinkle and crack on a man's body where it could cake up.

Me and my partner, Randall Bozworth Tatum, raised our tent's side flaps, and tried to enjoy a bit of refuge from the blistering sunlight and dense humid air—air that had the seeming power to suck all the life right out of a man. Our private site, which Boz referred to as The Viper's Nest, was part of Ranger Company B's command center out on the Trinity River north of Fort Worth. At least a hundred men in camp at times, but that day, couldn't have been more than twenty or thirty.

My partner and I made courageous, but losing, efforts at trying to get some rest after a month of beating the briars and brambles around Abilene in search of a wife-killer named Chauncy Pepperdine. Chauncy had taken an ax to the poor woman, and chopped her into four roughly equal pieces, after an argument over a less-than-tasty plate of biscuits and gravy she fixed for his supper. My God, biscuits and gravy. Damned amazing what people will kill one another over. Never did find the picky son of a bitch.

Heard later, Chauncy got his very own self murdered to death by an angry whore over in El Paso. Story went as how he tried to shortchange her after an extended night of raucous sex and whiskey-swilling pleasure. She jammed a six-inch bowie knife into his neck—all the way down to the bone handle. Pulled up a chair and watched him bleed out, right there in her rumpled bed. Everybody who knew Pepperdine felt God took care of the sorry son of a bitch's sinful ways, and figured that whore's brutal method of execution was simply good riddance.

Think I'd just managed to drift into a uncomfortably clammy nap when our commanding officer, Captain Wag Culpepper, summoned us to his pavilion. Wag wore his fancy full-blown English naval officer's outfit that morning. Gold braid, brass buttons, red sash, and all. He even strapped an impressive CSA cavalry sword around his stout waist. My guess was he wanted to make sure me and Boz left his rough office duly impressed with the gravity of whatever he had in mind as an assignment.

Our scruffy behinds had barely hit the canvas camp chairs, arranged in front of Wag's Civil War-surplus field desk, when he thumped ashes from a smoldering panatela, slapped the tabletop, and growled, "I have, this very morning, received word from my good friend Sheriff Andrew Cobb of San Augustine that he has captured Jackson Toefield. Want you boys to stroll over Cobb's way. Bring the murdering bastard back for trial and suitable hanging."

Boz snatched the palm-leaf sombrero from his sweat-drenched head and used it to whack at the layer of fine dust covering the sleeve of his faded bib-front shirt. He said, "Toefield's a bad 'un, Wag. What if he wuz to make a break for freedom, or accidentally get loose and beat the hell out of me and Lucius, or God forbid, kill one of us? Worthless stack of hammered meadow muffins is fully capable of it."

Culpepper eyeballed my partner like one of those bug collectors examining a newly discovered kind of beetle on a pin. He smiled and said, "Well, Boz, you'd probably have to shoot him. Wouldn't you?"

"Just wanted to make sure you didn't have your heart dead set on a hanging, what might not occur should I find it necessary to put eight or nine holes in the guest of honor," Boz said.

"Can I ask a question?" They'd left me totally in the dark, and I needed a mite more in the way of information. "Exactly who is Jackson Toefield, and why do we want to hang him?"

Culpepper shifted his grizzly-sized bulk into a more upright and imposing position. Blew a smoke ring the size of a washbasin my direction. "Well, Lucius, about six months before you joined up with us, Toefield got into an argument at one of the green-felt gaming tables in a now-defunct Hell's Half-Acre gambling parlor over in Fort Worth."

Boz jumped in and added, "Seems he didn't like the way his luck fell out. Heated exchanges involved hidden cards, dealin' seconds, shaved decks, and other such mouthy trash. Ole Jackson wasn't armed at the time. When he huffed out of the place, everyone in attendance at that particular prayer meeting thought he'd retired for the evening and was headed to the midnight singalong, revival, and free meal down at the rescue mission."

Our captain looked irritated at the interruption of his tale and boomed, "But their judgment proved faulty, and deadly. Toefield returned, in less than a minute, carrying a double-barreled coach gun loaded with buckshot. Splattered the dealer, and three other deacons at the table, all over the back wall of Bucky Greeb's Tin Pin Saloon. Hell of a goddamned mess. Place emptied out quicker'n a galvanized bucket in a drought."

Not to be denied his chance at the least contribution, Boz kept going like the tale belonged to him. "Before anyone had nerve enough to go back inside, Toefield disappeared like a puff of smoke in a cyclone."

Culpepper held a quieting finger in Boz's face and said, "Greeb posted a two-thousand-dollar bounty on the murderous slug's sorry hide. Naturally, that offer is probably null and void now. Bucky's business went straight to hell faster than small-town gossip at a church social, and never recovered. He closed the Tin Pin, left town seeking more lucrative opportunities, and has been gone for more than a year."

Boz threw his head back and snorted. "Guess Toefield ain't worth much these days, except maybe the entertainment of buying an ear of smoked corn on the cob and watchin' his sorry ass swing from the nearest tree limb."

Culpepper snapped, "Well, Boz, all your philosophical musings on future executions are neither here nor there. Once you've got that gob of spit shackled hand and foot, in custody, and are headed back this way, I want you to swing over to Iron Bluff on the Angelina River."

This unexpected ingredient in the mix threw me into a serious puzzlement. I glanced over at Boz. Man looked like someone had jerked his pants down and dropped a rabid weasel in his drawers.

He ran a damp palm from forehead to chin and moaned, "Why would you want us to stop in that Redlands hellhole, Horatio?" Use of the captain's given name by a close and trusted associate brought a new, and more serious, element to the discussion.

"The Redlands, you say? Us wet-behind-the-ears Waco natives must have led pretty sheltered lives. Never heard the term. Where is it?" I asked.

Boz kind of dismissively waved in my general direction. "Aw, it's just a big chunk of east Texas, from about Shelbyville south. Folks called it the Neutral Zone before Texas became a state. Most of the soil over there's that foot-stickin' red stuff. Town of Iron Bluff sits on a rust-colored piece about two hundred feet above the river. Never been over that way, huh, Lucius?"

"Passed through just ahead of a posse when my family vacated Louisiana. Our migration occurred so long ago, I don't really remember it."

Water-starved cottonwood leaves rustled underfoot on a blistering breeze as our bearlike leader frowned and leaned back. The dilapidated canvas chair complained from the stress as Culpepper twisted in his seat and tapped nervous fingers on the desktop. Took him almost a minute more of contemplative thought before he got around to answering Boz's original question.

Finally, he stood, moved to a spot less than arm's length from my partner, and said, "My brother's stepdaughter stopped in San Augustine, on the way back from her New Orleans school for genteel young ladies, almost three months ago. Initial correspondence led the family to believe she'd taken a teaching position in Lone Pine—a peckerwood-sized community ten miles south of Iron Bluff. Her letters stopped more'n a month ago. We're very concerned, Boz. Since I couldn't send you out on my own personal private business, Toefield's capture simply occurred at a most opportune time."

He rested a trembling hand on Boz's shoulder. "There's no one else I would trust with such a responsibility. We've been close friends for over twenty years. Need your help, old friend. I know you'll ferret out what has transpired with the girl, and return her to the bosom of a desperately concerned family, if at all possible."

"She got a name, Cap'n?" Both men turned my direction.

On the way back to his chair, Culpepper said, "Ruby Black. Can't miss this woman when you see her, Lucius. Quite possibly the most beautiful female in Texas. Blazing red hair, blue-eyed, and feisty as hell."

Being a man of action, who didn't take well to loafing around The Viper's Nest with nothing much to do, Boz jumped at the opportunity to hit the trail and get out on the prowl again. Man loved sleeping on the ground under an open sky more than anyone I've ever known.

He stood and said, "When do you want us to leave, Cap?"

"Tomorrow morning. I've already arranged a fully equipped mule for your trip. You might need to buy a few necessaries. Personal stuff mainly. At the very least, it's a two-hundred-mile trip. You'll be living in the open for a week or more." Culpepper looked burdened with concern when he added, "My brother and his wife are distraught. Don't think I've ever known a child loved like this one. I'd appreciate it if you'd get word to me as soon as you know anything useful, Boz."

"You have my oath on it, Wag. Any way under God's blue heaven, me and Lucius will get her back home."

"Always knew you would, Boz, but be careful, old friend. You know what it's like over that way. Easy to get dead in Iron Bluff."

2

"GONNA CUT YOUR NOSE AND EARS OFF"

WE SET OUT from Fort Worth before good light. My anxious partner took the lead, and set the pace. He didn't work himself into anything like a rush. Kind of moseyed along, and enjoyed the increasingly greener, and somewhat cooler, rolling woodlands of east Texas.

For the most part we kept clear of towns along the way. But Boz had a serious tobacco habit. The man smoked cigarettes as fast as he could roll them. Always felt he would've smoked a crowbar if he could've lit it. Most times he fired a new coffin nail off the dying one. Didn't take long before he ran low on papers, tobacco, matches, and every other thing imaginable to feed his habit. So we headed for Tyler.

I found me a chair out front of a place named Gillam's Mercantile. Dropped into it and tried to catch myself a little siesta while Boz shopped.

Ain't that just the way of things? Try to mind your own

business, maybe sneak a few winks on the side when you can, and what happens? Botheration comes and finds you. Seeks you out. Trouble is like that, you know. Just when you think life, the world, and the future are going along smoother than a newborn baby's rump, mayhem shows up and throws an iron bar right into the middle of everything.

I'd barely managed to relax a bit when a man with a voice that sounded like a bull snake hissing stopped in the street and said, "Well, I'll just be damned. There really is an all-seeing diety in heaven. He done let me find the one and only Lucius "By God" Dodge."

Heavily armed nimrod, a good head taller than me, swayed in the street like a split-trunked cottonwood tree in a heavy wind. Greasy black hair sprouted from beneath his ragged plainsman's hat. He held a quart-sized whiskey bottle in one hand and stroked the butt of a walnut-gripped Colt with the other.

Studied his twisted face for a spell before I recognized the scurvy dog. Hadn't seen the evil son of a bitch in almost three years, and harbored some difficulty placing who he was. His scraggly beard threw me off for a second or so. But less-than-fond recollection of his worthless soul finally came creeping back to the forefront of my memory.

"Well, now, I do believe we've got the renowned Hangtown Johnny Crusher here in the flesh. Thought me and Boz put your ugly ass in prison, Johnny. If memory serves, the judge said you were supposed to be away for at least five years."

"Judges don't know ever-goddamned-thang, Dodge. Neither do you." His rasping voice sounded like spit on a hot stove lid. He upended the bottle and took a long sloppy swig. Some of the liquid fire dribbled around cracked lips into his disheveled beard.

"Have you made any effort to behave, Johnny? I surely

wouldn't want to send you back down to Huntsville for another stint of chopping cotton and picking peas for the state."

"Ain't going back to no damned prison. Done picked my last batch of vegetables. Do as I goddamned please now—and forever more." He took a whack at the bottle and slobbered, "And today it pleases me to kill the hell out of you, Dodge."

Always found it difficult, at best, to pull a pistol when sitting. So, I eased myself out of the chair as slowly as I could. "No need for such drastic measures on a hot day like this, Johnny. I'd rather not work up a sweat over nothing, if you wouldn't mind. Our business was finished a long time ago. Why don't you just get over it and move along," I said.

"Why don't you go to hell? Better yet, why don't I send you there? Get your sorry self out here in the street where I can see you, Dodge. Gonna enjoy blastin' a few holes in your worthless hide. Soon as you're dead, gonna cut your nose and ears off. Make myself a necklace out of 'em."

I stepped off the boardwalk and into the street. We couldn't have been more than ten feet apart. Hangtown Johnny was so saturated with bootleg nose paint I could smell him. Man could barely stand. Tried one more time to dissuade him from making another, and perhaps last, bad decision in a lifetime of them.

"Best thing for you would be to find a nice shady spot and sleep it off before this goes any further, Johnny. You're in no shape to swap shots with anyone today."

"Piss on you, Dodge. Soon as you're dead, think I'll do exactly that. Finish off this fine bottle of day-old hooch, then, once you're in the ground, I'll christen your passage to the other side. You'll hit Satan's front doorstep smellin' exactly the way you look."

"That's your problem, Johnny. Right now you're *not* thinking straight. Whiskey's burned up your brain."

"Had plenty of time for thinkin' in that 'ere prison cell, you badge-totin' bastard. Still cain't believe you and Tatum sent me down for killing that bag of puss George Talbot. Son of a bitch sold me a blind horse." He sucked down another slobber-drenched hit off his bottle and went back to his rant. "Then the motherless son of a whore wouldn't give my money back. I had to kill 'em. Tried to do it 'fore he told anyone what a fool he'd made out of me. Scum-suckin' weasel made me look stupid 'fore my friends."

I'd heard all I wanted. Have to admit I provoked him a bit with, "You *are* stupid, Johnny. I've known ten-year-old jackasses smarter than you."

Walnut-brained churnhead's eyes bugged. He made a sound like he was strangling and went for his pistol, but the tubful of firewater he'd consumed got between a liquor-logged brain and his hand. My first shot hit him in the left side just above the spot where he'd shoved the pistol in his belt. Spun him around like a kid's top. Lucky skunk surprised hell out of me when he sent one sizzling past my right ear.

Figured I'd best get serious, before he went and landed a lucky one somewhere in my hide. Put my next shot in his chest about an inch right of his breastbone. Massive chunk of lead knocked him backward three or four feet. Saw the soles of his boots when he flipped up and landed on his shoulders. Geyser of hot blood spurted from the hole. Be damned if the whiskey saturated no-account didn't sit up, take a swig from his bottle, and rip off another one that knocked the heel off my boot.

By that point, black powder and sudden death set screaming women and bawling kids to running in every direction. In the corner of my eye, I spotted Boz as he jumped from Gillam's porch with a flame-and-smoke-spitting pistol in each hand. He must have put half-a-dozen holes in Hangtown Johnny faster than I could count them. Poor shot-to-pieces fool flopped around in the street like someone was beating on him with a long-handled shovel.

When the thunderous blasting from Boz's pistols finally stopped, he turned and said, "You hit, son?"

"No, but for a man who's most likely bleeding hundred-and-fifty-proof gator sweat, ole Hangtown gave it a helluva try."

We ambled over to the body. Johnny still had the bottle in his hand. Honest to God, it looked like he was trying to take the last swig before going out.

"What the hell happened, Lucius?"

"Not sure, Boz. He was drunk, crazed, and mad 'cause we sent him to prison. Said he was gonna kill me, cut my nose and ears off, and piss on my grave. You know how the man was. Never could stop picking at a scab till he turned it back into a sore spot."

Boz holstered one of his weapons, and began reloading the other. "Got enough lead in him now to make a set of horseshoes. Hell of a waste, but some men just won't let a thing loose when they get to ragging around on bad memories. Gotta put this behind us, Lucius. Try not to dwell on it much."

"Needn't trouble yourself, Boz. He called death down on his own head, far as I'm concerned. Tried to talk the silly bastard out of pulling on me. Think he'd decided to die long before this morning."

Local constabulary strolled over and expressed some serious concerns about stand-up shootings on their city's main street. They held pretty earnest reservations about such matters. Didn't care for Rangers who rode into their nice quiet town and got into a pistol fight that scared hell out of everyone, from the mayor to the bar swamp in a nearby saloon.

Mayor bustled in on the conversation. He fumed, fussed,

and blathered some too. Think maybe there was an election coming up. Citizens stood around and nodded their agreement to most of what he yammered on about. Typical kind of thing you come to expect from people who've just had the bejabbers scared out of them. But hell, the killing wasn't our fault.

Marshal finally came over to our side of the disagreement, after Boz thoroughly explained the situation. We managed to get out of town later that afternoon, but only after consenting to leave enough money to pay for Hangtown Johnny's interment. Mortician gave us what he claimed was a cut rate. Boz said later we'd paid enough to have a draft horse buried. Turned south at the first opportunity and headed for Nacogdoches. It was but a short ride of less than forty miles from there to our destination.

Boz and I'd started our Ranger partnership nigh onto eighteen months prior to the San Augustine raid. Over time, I'd learned that once he got himself away from civilization, he wouldn't return until absolutely necessary. Man drew an uncommon amount of strength from living in the wilds and sleeping under God's own roof on a bed of straw.

Didn't matter one way or the other where we slept. But Boz always tried for spots near a creek or river, in the hope that nights would prove a shade cooler and more bearable.

Weather went from hot to brutal hot once the sun was up, and usually turned cloudy in the evenings. Lightning-spiked blue-black skies invariably promised cooling rain that never came. Clouds disappeared after dark, mostly. The grinding buzz from locusts that droned deep into the night grew to a dull roar. Damned bugs had the ability to keep the weariest traveler from getting much in the way of sleep. On top of everything else, growing suspicions about our mission led me to spend most of my waking moments in preparation for gunplay more intense than anything Hangtown Johnny could have imagined on his best day.

Captain Culpepper bore responsibility for my marked uneasiness of mind. Boz added to it, one night, when we'd stretched out beside a free-flowing stream that actually provided some relief from our sufferings.

Racket from the locusts let up a bit and I asked, "Why'd you call Iron Bluff a hellhole?"

He let the question hover over us for a minute or so before he said, "May have been the wrong selection of words on my part, Lucius. It's not exactly the kind of town you'd normally bring to mind when you hear a place described in such a manner. Ain't none of the street-walking whores or brazen lawlessness that usually involves robbery, rape, senseless murder, and such. But make no mistake, son, there's been plenty of murder done there anyway."

"That doesn't make any sense, Boz. What's the difference between senseless murder and just plain murder?"

"Bad blood, Lucius, bad blood. See, 'bout ten years ago, a feller name of Bull Tingwell moved his brood onto a piece of land up on the Angelina, just north of town."

"Nothing wrong with that."

"Nope. Not a thing. Story I've heard people tell says he bought all the property available at the time. Then, he put his ranch buildings between the river and a family name of Pitt, who'd settled their plot back when Texas was still a republic."

"Well, now, that sounds like people looking for trouble."

"That it does. Ole Man Pitt and his bunch considered themselves akin to landed gentry. Kind of like lords of the Redlands. Highly refined bunch, according to the stories I've heard. They deemed Tingwell and his clan as less than human and closer to being the two-legged relatives of armadillos or skunks."

"Did the families not get along from the very outset?"

"Not for certain sure, Lucius. Just know that, 'bout a year after the Tingwells' arrival, folks from both sides started going at each other's throats—and haven't let up. State of affairs seems to have started out as bullying fist-fights between their kids that graduated to gunfire pretty quick. Most travelers, aware of the area's history, avoid the town. Rumors I've heard would lead a wary man to believe members of either bunch will grab up a stranger for consideration if no one else is available."

"You said there'd been killings."

"Well, both tribes started out with three sons. Oldest one of the Tingwell boys was a brute called Buster. Way I heard it, ole Buster took uncommon pleasure from beating the hell out of just about anyone he could latch onto. Seems he made it his mission in life to find one of the Pitt boys any-time he felt an urge to exercise a set of fists the size of ham hocks. Seems he was 'specially attracted to the oldest of the Pitt boys. Kid named Albert. Buster and Albert were only eight or nine years old when it all started. Sparrin' around went on for years and the older Buster got, the meaner he got."

"God Almighty, but I do hate a bully. Childhood bullies can stay with you for the rest of your life, Boz."

"Well, Buster didn't get a chance to stay in the hearts and minds of too many of those he'd beat the hell out of for very long."

"What does that mean?"

"Friends of mine, from over this way, told me he'd whipped the snot out of the whole county for most of his life. Paid special weekly attention to Albert Pitt. Then, someone caught Buster out on the Shelbyville Road a little 'fore sundown one afternoon, and put enough buckshot in his back to make a boat anchor, two or three anvils, and a plow. Reloaded—and shot him some more. Corpse was barely recognizable when his family went looking and found him a day or so later."

"Hot damn, Boz. Sounds like Albert Pitt had had all the ass-whipping he wanted."

"Generally accepted opinion expressed by most of Nacogdoches County at the time, Lucius. Not certain I believe it myself. If I heard all the stories correctly, Albert never evidenced the kind of personality, grit, or downright meanness necessary for a back-shooter."

Boz stopped the tale long enough to pull a cigar from his pocket and light up. Fished around in one of our supply bags and found a bottle, then poured us both a healthy dram and settled back into his nest.

Light from a glowing full moon, the size of a Number 10 washtub, played off the nearby water. Looked almost like midday, even under the monstrous, rustling cotton-wood where we'd dropped our gear.

"Don't know, Boz. Always felt you could push any man just so far. You hurt him enough and, eventually, he'll make you pay a heavy price for your pleasure."

Boz sipped at his cup, drew a lungful of dense smoke, and mumbled, "Maybe."

"Puts me in mind of a kid I knew in Waco who got similar treatment from a local bully named Pottsy Hancock. Poor boy put up with weekly beatings from Pottsy for two or three years. Finally, one day, the bully showed up ready for his fun, but the intended victim pulled a butcher's knife out of his pants."

"A butcher's knife? Strange weapon for a child."

"Damned big one too. Stuck it in Pottsy's thigh, just below his belt. Wounded jackass let out a yelp that sounded like a gut-shot panther. He tried to run. Damaged leg slowed him down considerable. Way I heard it, the kid poked him in the ass about twenty times. Ole Pottsy slept on his stomach for six months. Poor bastard had trouble going to the outhouse for more than a year. Never bullied another person, though, far as I know."

By that point, Boz'd laughed himself into a hacking cough. He sat up to take a medicinal sip from his cup and said, "Well, that might be true of your friend from Waco, but I still don't think Albert was the guilty party in Buster Tingwell's murder. Don't matter what I think, though. Three weeks after Buster bit the dirt, Albert floated to the surface of the Angelina River, right below the Tingwells' ranch."

"Murdered?"

"Coroner's inquest in Nacogdoches ruled his death an accident. Don't believe that steaming pile of horseshit either."

"Damn, Boz. What *do* you believe?"

He sipped, puffed, and mulled my question over for so long, I got to wondering whether he intended on ever turning loose of an answer.

Finally, my friend sighed, sucked down another stiff swallow of his drink, and said, "I've always felt Albert's brother, Eli, kilt Buster, and the two remaining Tingwell boys knew it. But were so afraid of Eli, they drowned Albert instead. Easier man to kill."

"Been getting worse over the years, huh?"

"Absolutely. Since Albert's passing, both families have hired a number of gunmen, and there's been several more killings. Their dispute ain't festered to a full-time feud yet but mark my word, it's simply a matter of time and place. Trust me on this one, Lucius. Steppin' in the middle of family feuds can get you killed graveyard dead plenty pronto."

He rolled over, crushed his smoke in the dirt, and pitched the remaining liquor out on the ground. "That's why we're gonna gather Toefield up from San Augustine's sheriff, and then go visit an old friend of mine who lives nearby. Need more'n the two of us if we want to go rattlin' cages around these parts."

San Augustine's Sheriff Cobb was happier than a two-tailed dog to see us. Even more pleased to get rid of his less-than-favorite prisoner. Didn't take long to understand why.

Toefield spent almost every waking moment whining about everything from his meals— ". . . ain't never enough on my plate. You bastards is tryin' to starve me to death. Been weaker'n a baby lamb ever since I got locked up . . ."—to the number of trips he was allowed to the out-house— ". . . let me the hell out of here. 'Bout to explode. If 'n somebody don't get me to the facilities, I'll turn this cell into a real stink hole."

We thanked Cobb for his historic patience and sense of duty. Loaded Toefield onto the mule with our cash of stores. Course he didn't like it much. "Damnation, cain't you Ranger bastards afford another horse? Why in hellfire does I have to ride this bony-backed mule? Shit, this is hellacious uncomfortable. Ain't one of you boys got a blanket I can set on?"

Boz pulled his Winchester, leaned over, and rapped Toefield on the noggin with the barrel. He didn't hit the man with any real enthusiasm. Just enough of a smack to get his attention. Prisoner yelped like he'd been struck by a falling anvil.

Boz said, "Stop that racket, or I'll whack you again."

"You didn't have to hit me. You badge-carryin' son of a bitch."

Sure enough, Boz whacked him again. Bit more passion in that second lick. Raised a nice bump. Even bled some. Toefield rubbed at the knot while his lip quivered and his face twisted into a mask of feigned pain.

Barely heard Boz when he said, "I'm a right affable

feller, Jack. Love peace and quiet too. You start with this pissin' and moanin' again and, I swear, you'll arrive in Fort Worth with so many bumps on that melon-thick head of yours, folks will think you've got some form of hideous new medical ailment." He turned and started to move us out, but stopped and said, "Oh, by the way. If you jackrabbit on me, I will kill you."

I tried like hell not to laugh—only partially succeeded. Toefield glared at me like he would have taken great pleasure in pulling all the hairs out of my nose—one at a time. The notion just made me laugh that much harder.

3

"Poor Man's A-Laying on the Boardwalk, All Bloody and Dying"

BOZ LED OUR three-man parade east through San Augustine to an almost nonexistent village called Thorn's Corners. We headed off the road and into the piney woods, on the other side of a whitewashed church. Rustic house of worship was one of only five buildings in evidence. It sat next to a disreputable-looking saloon that appeared to have predated the church by a number of years. Suppose the odd proximity of religion and whiskey worked for the natives.

We must have gone another two miles before our guide stopped at a neatly laid-out log house, surrounded by equally well-kept outbuildings and corrals. No flowers planted out front or any other evidence of a woman's presence, though.

A man the size of a Butterfield stagecoach stepped onto the porch. Long-barreled shotgun rested across his left arm. He shouted, "You fellers have business here?"

Boz yelled back, "Put your weapons away, Rip. It's Boz Tatum."

Smile like a barn door flashed across the man's face. He lowered his ten-gauge blaster and placed it inside the door. Few seconds later, he and Boz hugged and slapped one another on the back like long-lost brothers home from the Civil War. An abundance of laughter and friendly joshing around followed.

Good God, but the man was even bigger up close. Most folks considered me a nice-sized feller. Stood over six feet tall in my stockings back then. But Boz Tatum's friend towered over me like a brick, two-story Dallas bank building.

Boz said, "This youngster's my Ranger partner, Lucius Dodge, Rip. Lucius, shake hands with Ripley Thorn." My hand disappeared into Thorn's like I'd shoved it into a bushel basket.

"Friends call me Rip, Boz. You know that. Right pleased to make your acquaintance, Lucius. Anyone who can travel with a south Texas skunk like Boz Tatum has to be of exceptional breeding and tolerance." Thorn roared with laughter at his own joke, and poked Boz on the shoulder again.

Boz faked a painful wince, then pointed at our captive. "Jackass ridin' the mule is a prisoner in transit to Fort Worth. Name's Toefield. Don't let him get started complaining. Man has the power to melt your ears with all his bellyaching and whining. Sheriff in San Augustine done went and lost both of his 'cause of Toefield."

Thorn grinned. "You can put a stop to such as that with a rifle barrel. Seen you do it before."

"He's already applied the rifle barrel remedy," I said. "Toefield hasn't uttered a word since we left San Augustine. Been right peaceful."

An arm the size of a tree trunk swept around Boz's shoulders. "Hell, you ain't changed a bit, old friend. Shackle that

piece of scum to the iron ring hanging out of that oak over
yonder, Boz, and come on inside. We'll uncork a bottle. Talk
about old times. Figure out why you've turned up in my tiny-
assed corner of Texas heaven."

The inside of Thorn's house appeared as neatly kept as
the outside. Might not have been a woman about, but you
couldn't tell it from the clean, and carefully arranged, interior of the rough log building.

Our host seated us at a store-bought table, brought out a
jug of locally cooked corn squeezings, poured each of us a
large tin cup, and surprised me when he took one out to
Toefield. Laughed when he came back and said our chastised prisoner almost cried over his display of kindness.

Took the two old amigos about half an hour to relive
their Rangering days. They told hair-raising tales of fighting Comanches, and stories of bad men, bad women, and
bad places. Laughed heartily at good times gone, and almost wept at the mention of close friends killed in the line
of duty.

Eventually, the conversation got around to the question I
knew had nibbled at the edges of Thorn's mind since the
second he recognized Boz in front of his home. "What's up,
boys? Don't get many visitors out this way. Figure you must
have something other than good times gone, dead com-
padres, and discussin' the merits of the foggy past in mind."

Boz went through all the reasons we'd made our trip, including the possible disappearance of Captain Culpepper's
niece. Then added, "Figured you likely had as much, or
more, knowledge of the Tingwell-Pitt situation in Iron
Bluff as anyone in these parts, and just might be bored
enough of putterin' around this place to come along with
us. Three men are always better'n two, no matter how you
slice it. And when I'm about to step in a cow pie the size of
this one, I want men I can trust beside me."

"Well, I ain't so sure of that'n, Boz. Hell, if I had a part-ner what carried as many pistols as young Lucius Dodge here, don't think I'd be afraid of anything. How many of them '73 Colt poppers you got, son? Counted three on your person so far, plus that meat cleaver of a bowie."

"One on each hip. One behind. Carry four black-powder Dragoons in the pommel holsters on Grizz. Plus a Win-chester model '76 and a twelve-gauge coach gun. Got a lit-tle boot knife down here, and a four-shot derringer in my shirt pocket. That's all."

"That's all, huh? Should be enough for just about any kind of skirmish in these parts, and you're very likely gonna need the whole pile of 'em. Jesus, I feel for your poor horse. Hellacious load of iron he's carrying."

"Don't worry yourself, Rip. My blue roan is more than up to the task."

Things got quiet for a spell. Thorn caressed his flowing beard and looked thoughtful. "The Tingwells and Pitts are moving closer to all-out war with every day that passes, Boz. Friend of mine lives in Lone Pine. I get a report from him almost every week. He's plenty worried. Last missive I received mentioned a possible move to some other part of the state. Think his exact words were 'somewhere a long ways from here.' Not sure where he'd go, but I wouldn't be surprised to discover he'd already skedaddled."

I leaned into the conversation and asked, "What's he so afraid of, Rip?"

"Well, in the beginning, it was only the kids that were scrapping around. You know, school fights and such. Then a couple of 'em got dead. After Albert Pitt unexpect-edly and mournfully drowned, his pappy, Romulus, went out and hired a McLennan County gunfighter name of Nick Fox. I heard Bull Tingwell almost had a stroke when he found out what Romulus did. So he scouted around and employed a murderous gunman from down Gonzales way."

"Fox was bad enough. Who'd Tingwell hire?" Boz sounded like a man looking up from the bottom of his own grave.

Thorn's gaze dropped to his empty cup. He scratched his head, sighed, and said, "You ain't gonna like this at all, Boz."

"Damn, Rip. Go ahead. Gimme the whole badger— teeth, claws, hair, eyeballs, and all. I want the entire ugly beast. We've been friends for long enough that you know I hate to be teased like this."

The big man blurted, "John Roman Hatch, Boz. Old Man Tingwell's got John Roman Hatch ridin' by his side. And both families have even gone so far as to take on four or five minor belligerent types for the coming fight. Way I've got it figured, one of these days, someone's gonna shuffle the cards, the joker will get turned up, and when it does the Angelina will instantly become the bloodiest river in the Redlands."

Boz closed his eyes. "Sweet Jesus. This trip is rapidly turning into a nightmare. Reckon it'd be all right for us to wish we was somewhere else too. Anywheres else but the place we now find ourselves." He absentmindedly pulled one of his pistols and rolled the cylinder around with his thumb. I heard him barely breathe, "Sweet Jesus. John Roman Hatch."

I moved even closer to Rip and whispered, "Tell me about Hatch. Who is he?"

Thorn threw me a sheepish grin. "South Texas *pistolero*. Got his start killin' cattle thieves for some of the larger landholders down that way during the Yankee Reconstruction. Worked for them bastards in the state police for a spell too. Graduated to general murder of anyone what crossed his gore-soaked path, and other forms of bloody mayhem over the years. Not a man to be trifled with, Lucius."

"Any way to recognize Hatch, should I run on him and neither of you boys is around?" I asked.

Rip said, "Cain't miss him. Fancy dresser. Given to blood-red silk vests, black hats trimmed in silver. Favors them knee-high cavalry boots. Keeps 'em polished up like black bone. Likes them big ole Mexican spurs too. Rowels the size of ten-dollar gold pieces."

Boz shook his head like a man amazed. "He once shot a feller in a Mexican cantina just for having one eye. Hatch said anyone that ugly didn't deserve to live. Course Nick Fox ain't no slouch in the killing business either."

Rip pushed his chair back on two legs, sipped at the cup, then said, "I've heard tell he'll kill a feller just to see the look of surprise on the man's face as his limp body drops into the dust. Least them's the stories I've heard."

Boz said, "Wonder if Wag knew about this. Can't believe the man would send us over here knowing what you just told me, Rip. Good God Almighty, a pair of killers like the ones you just mentioned, along with their cohorts, could be a handful for a whole company of Rangers."

Thorn threw his head back and laughed. "Hell, Boz. You know the old sayin' well as I do. Don't need but one Ranger, no matter what the situation. Tribe of wild Indians killin' folks in obscene ways, send a Ranger. Riots in the streets, send a Ranger. Armies of gunfighters in Iron Bluff, send Ranger Randall Bozworth Tatum. He'll get the job done. Whatever you want, friends and neighbors. Ole Boz can do it. If Boz cain't, who in hell can?"

I said, "Ain't there any law in Iron Bluff?"

"Sure. They's town marshals in Iron Bluff and Lone Pine both. Lone Pine's got a damned good 'un. He keeps his tiny piece of heaven reined in pretty tight. Gunmen from both camps tend to stay away from Frank Tuttle's town. Rumors are Romulus Pitt owns the one in Iron Bluff.

Couldn't testify to that myself, but I have my suspicions."

"You gonna go with us, Rip?" Boz's question kinda brought Thorn up short.

His huge paw enveloped the tin cup as he drained the fiery contents. Wiped a dripping chin and snapped, "Hell, yes, I'm goin' with you. Wouldn't miss this dance for a bucketful of newly minted gold coin. Be real interestin' to see how John Roman Hatch reacts when he realizes the Texas Rangers are after his worthless, murderin' hide. Real interestin'. Besides, you boys get kilt, who else besides me gonna burry you. Gonna have to go along just to make sure I don't have to dig two graves."

"Good to hear it, old friend. Cap'n Culpepper sent papers and a badge for you just to take care of the legalities. Got 'em outside in my pouch."

Two days later, the four of us moseyed along the wagon road about half a mile from Lone Pine. Trees grew right up to the edge of the rutted path. In some places limbs, heavy with leaves and badly in need of water, drooped almost to the ground under the weight of rapidly browning greenery. Made seeing more than a hundred yards ahead almost impossible.

Our mule, and one of Rip's, plodded behind. Toefield couldn't have been happier. A kindhearted Ripley Thorn had provided the murdering slug with his own horse to ride. Suppose a couple of raps on the noggin, and a compliant animal, settled pretty much all his problems on this earth, 'cause we didn't hear another word of complaint out of the man. He got so quiet for a spell, set me to thinking Boz might have hit him a little harder than I thought. Maybe knocked something loose in his thinker box. Boz loved the peace and quiet.

We'd stopped in the middle of the road for a quick drag on our canteens when this towheaded kid, who looked about twelve or thirteen years old, ran up and squeaked, "Don't go into town, fellers. Some bad fellers just shot Marshal Tuttle in front of the bank. Poor man's a-layin' on the boardwalk, all bloody and dying. Them killers is inside the bank now robbin' hell out of everyone." Tried to stop him, but he'd heeled it for the safety of the sheltering woods before I could open my mouth.

Boz didn't waste any time deciding what to do. "Rip, you stay here with Toefield and the animals. Me and Lucius will see to this."

Thorn pulled his pistol and said, "Damned if you're leaving me behind with a pair of mules and a shackled killer. I'm a-going along. Kid said they's bad fellers done the killin'. Sounds like more'n one to me. You might need my help. Besides, done told you I want to be in on the whole shooting match. Only way to make sure you boys stay alive."

Boz blinked about twice and redirected his attention at Toefield. "Remember what I said to you in San Augustine about doing a rabbit on me?"

Toefield scrunched down in the saddle like he'd been slapped across the mouth. "Yessir. Ain't about to forget anytime soon."

"What'd I say?"

"Said you'd kill the hell out of me."

"Good answer, Jack. Gonna leave you here with the mules. Soon as we're out of sight, you follow us on into town. You run, and I'll keep my promise. Understand?"

"Yessir. Be a-following right along with the mules, Mr. Tatum, suh."

We put the spur to our animals and, in a few minutes,

pulled up beside a sign on the edge of town. Carved into a rough pine plank mounted on a heavy post was LONE PINE-POP. 237. Third line read, LEAVE YOUR GUNS WITH THE MARSHAL.

Whole community didn't amount to much more'n a wide spot in the road. Nothing but a church, saloon, bank, general store, small hotel, livery, barbershop, and not much else. Typical, back in them days, for a small town that'd probably be gone in a dozen years or less. All the buildings were arranged, hit and miss, on either side of the wagon road that split the village in half.

Draped half on and half off the boardwalk, right in front of the bank's door, a nicely dressed gentleman oozed his life into the hard-packed red soil. Rip said, "That's Frank Tuttle all right. Probably the nattiest man in these parts. Looks pretty well played out from here."

We could hear yelling behind the heavy glass that made up most of the entire front of the building. Other than Tuttle's leaking body, the rest of the village's only thoroughfare appeared deserted. Cautious citizens peeked from curtained windows opposite the action, but didn't appear willing to get drawn into whatever atrocity might be taking place in their bank.

When I mentioned a decided lack of involvement by locals, Rip said, "Frank Tuttle had 'em under a pretty heavy thumb. Man didn't allow no guns in town. He posted signs about checking your firearms on damn near every flat surface you can see. Be willing to bet most of their weapons are locked in a cell down at the jail."

We dismounted. Me and Boz pulled our shotguns and checked the loads. I fished more shells from my saddle pouch. Handed Boz about half a dozen, in case he needed them.

Dropped the last round in our leader's hand just as Rip said, "How you boys wanna handle this mess?"

Boz snapped his big popper shut. "I'll go round back. There's gotta be a door somewhere. You two wait out front till you hear me yellin'. Come in double quick. We get 'em going in more'n one direction at a time and, maybe, we can stop this with no bloodshed. If they decide to fight, try not to kill any civilians."

Rip chuckled. "Yeah. Guess it wouldn't look very good to rub out a passel of natives our first day in town."

"You really think this jumped-up plan is gonna work, Boz? At least one of 'em got smart enough to pull the shades. We don't have the slightest inkling where any of the thieving bastards are," I said.

Tatum stared at me like I'd lost my mind. "It'll work, Lucius. Don't care how bad a man might think he is, you get him starin' at the wrong end of a shotgun and he'll start gettin' religion right quick. Just do as I do when we get inside. Bet they'll give it up in less than a minute. But if they start anything wayward, kill 'em."

Still had my doubts. "Not sure 'bout this one, Boz. You know I'm the gamest puppy in the pit. So you lead on, big dog, but if any of these knot heads get to looking real stupid, or real serious, the nearest undertaker's gonna need a dustpan and a broom to pick them up."

He threw me an understanding grin, and darted around the nearest corner. Rip and I did our best Comanche tiptoe over to the heavy, glass-paned front door and waited. Had to step over Marshal Tuttle's blood-soaked body. Reached down and turned him over. Man surprised both of us when he moaned.

Rip pulled the wounded lawdog's suit coat aside, and lifted the edges of the shirt underneath. "Jesus, cain't believe he's still alive. Hole is mighty close to his heart. Looks like the slug missed any ribs, and came out his back. If this tough ole bird can hang on a bit longer, we just might be lookin' at a miracle, Lucius."

Lowered shades kept those inside from seeing us sneak up and flatten out against the door. Rip tried the knob. Shook his head. Locked. Sweat pooled up like a deep-water lake under my arms and ran into the top of my pants. Pulled my bandanna and dabbed at a dripping forehead. Even had to wipe the stock of the shotgun to get it dried off. Sun bored through my hat like a carpenter's auger.

About a minute after getting settled, we heard one hell of a wood-rending commotion and an uncommon amount of yelling. Rip hit the front door like a bull with a Roman candle up its ass. Big man knocked the heavy panel completely off the hinges. Oak splinters and glass shards flew around us like sweets from a busted piñata. For them folks inside, the scene must have looked like the door exploded.

I went in, snugged up behind my human battering ram. Almost stumbled over a woman and two fellers stretched out on the floor. Deposit slips, sheets of writing paper, and all manner of other debris floated on the air we'd stirred up with our door-busting entrance. Before you could say, "Hands up," we'd thrown down on some of the most surprised bank robbers who ever lived.

Boz couldn't have been any cooler than a skunk basking in December's icy moonlight. He had all three of those amateur stickup artists under the gun. They'd ganged up in front of the gold-accented safe, back behind a waist-high counter. From the looks of things, those poor stupid boys had spent most of their time since the robbery began trying to figure out how they might force the big beast open. Problem had proved an insurmountable mental exercise for the dim-witted bunch.

Heard one of them mutter, "Good God, they's Rangers."

Dumb son of a bitch who acted as their leader did have some monumental *huevos* on him, though. He looked us up and down, studied the open end of Boz's big blaster for a second or so, and snapped, "You Rangers throw them shotguns away, or I'll kill this banker man we done got down here on the floor, sure as chickens has feathers."

Chuckle that sounded like a bear growling kinda rumbled up from somewhere way down in Rip Thorn's chest right before he snarled, "Go ahead. None of us know 'im. We's gonna shoot bloody hell out of you boys anyhow, just for the by-God fun of it."

Place got real quiet. I could hear heavy breathing from the frightened patrons on their bellies behind me. My ears opened up bigger than the wheels on a chuck wagon. Bank clock ticked like someone beating on a metal washboard with a water dipper. Thieves got to sucking air so hard you'd a-thought they'd just run a footrace.

Poor banker man on the floor moaned, "Oh, God, please don't kill me. Told you, I'm just a teller. The owner's in San Augustine. Won't be back till later this afternoon. He's the only one with the combination."

Thief I had covered swung his pistol around from Boz, and zeroed in on me. When he cocked the damned thing, it sounded like someone rolled an anvil across the floor. Hard to believe the man did something so deadly stupid. Silly bastard couldn't have been ten feet away when I pulled the trigger and blasted him out of both boots. Concussion from the explosion deafened everyone in the building for about ten seconds. Fog bank of gun smoke rolled over the counter and made it right difficult to see too.

Dead man's partners in crime got a serious case of instant heartfelt religion. The newly converted threw their pistols all the way across the room, and hollered, "Sweet

Jesus," and, "Oh, my God, you kilt poor Harold," and, "He
wouldna harmed a fly," and, "God Almighty, please don't
be a-killin' us too."

Citizens laid out on the floor hopped up and headed
for the door. Woman hit the boardwalk first. She went
to screaming like a sawmill whistle at lunch. Kept the
screeching up all the way across the street, and into the
sheltering arms of concerned folks hiding in the local
mercantile.

Boz hopped over the counter, grabbed the thieving idiots still standing, and pushed them up against the wall. He
slapped all over both men looking for more weapons, but
didn't find a one.

Rip glanced at me like I'd just appeared out of thin air.
"By God, Dodge, thought you was just yammerin' outside
when you said what you did. Hell, I was a-trying to skeer
these ole boys a bit. Figured we could talk 'em into givin'
up. Didn't have any real intention of shootin' anyone."

Know now my words must have sounded harsh, but as I
pushed open the little gate in the counter and stepped into
the private area to keep our prisoners covered, I snapped,
"Best understand right now, I don't make idle threats, Rip.
Boz knows that better than anyone in Texas. You'll notice
he didn't even flinch when I popped that chucklehead.
Dumb bastard forfeited his life soon as he pointed his pistol my direction and cocked it."

Rip pushed past me, and toed at the dead man's crumpled
corpse. "Christ, you damn near blew this ole boy in half."

Took a few minutes before a formally dressed gent
showed up. He pushed his way through a small knot of
town folk who stood in the street and whispered behind
their hands.

The gaunt gentleman strode to the back of the bank.
Hesitantly moved toward the dead outlaw and, in an odd

disembodied voice, said, "My name is Gibbs Melton, Rangers. Town barber, dentist, and leader of the local religious community. I usually take care of the dead, when necessary."

Boz shook the man's extended hand, but looked a mite uncomfortable. "You got a doctor around these parts, Mr. Melton? Your marshal is still alive. Shot through and through, but perhaps savable." He pointed at my bloody handiwork and added, "This poor bastard here's deader'n Santa Anna. Marshal Tuttle might benefit a good deal more from your attention."

Lone Pine's barber/undertaker/soul-saver glanced over his shoulder toward the fractured door. "We've already moved Frank to the jail. Several of the town's concerned ladies are attending his wounds as we speak. Not really much we can do, except try to stop the bleeding and hope for the best. He's strong as an ox. We'll all beseech the Lord for his life."

Rip said, "May take considerable prayin' for the Lord to repair holes the size of them two, Reverend Melton. I like Frank as much as anyone, but he'd lost a bucket of blood by the time we got here."

"The Lord sees over of those who deserve it, sir. I'm sure there's plenty of room in the grand scheme of things to insure Marshal Tuttle's survival. In the meantime, this poor wretch needs to be placed in a coffin for burial. Hot as it is today, he'll ripen up in a matter of hours. Some of my congregation will attend to the cleansing of blood and innards from the wall and floor. Smell from such a mess tends to get rank pretty quick." He turned on his booted heel and glided away from us like a ghost.

Boz muttered, "You ever seen anything like him, Lucius? I've known more'n my share of undertakers and funeral directors. But by God, that 'un's the creepiest man

I've ever met. Makes my skin pimple and crawl like a plucked chicken's. Should anything wayward happen while we're here, don't let him touch me. Jesus, get a case of the icy shivers just thinking 'bout it."

4

"... Armed to the Teeth, and Lookin' Meaner'n Hell"

MARSHAL TUTTLE DIDN'T spend much time suffering in his jail. One of the ladies nursing the wounded lawman offered her bed in what we thought a right kindly gesture. Later, we discovered she and the marshal had recently struck up a close personal relationship that seemed to meet with the approval of everyone who attended their church.

Me, Boz, and Rip moved all our traps into Tuttle's newly abandoned lockup. Toefield raised holy hell when we tried to put him in with our surviving would-be bank robbers.

"I ain't no run-of-the-mill, sorry-assed criminal. I'm a murderer. Kilt four men on the same night. It ain't right to wedge a man of my lofty importance in with scruffy rabble like these bastards."

Rip leaned on the cell door and laughed. "You mean to tell me you're offended by the company of bank robbers?"

"These shit heels didn't rob no bank. Tried, but didn't succeed. They ain't no better'n watermelon-stealin' kids, far as I'm concerned. I'm a real honest-to-God man-killer, and should have my own cell. You got three empty, 'cept that'n with the checked guns in it. Ain't no point puttin' us in the one."

Hard to believe, but he sounded almost reasonable. Boz nodded his approval. Me and Rip took all the checked smoke wagons out of the barred compartment farthest from the door of the office and stacked them behind the marshal's desk. Wanted all that firepower as far away from the prisoners as possible. Moving the weapons left an empty cell between Toefield and the failed thieves. Appeared those boys were as glad to get rid of him as he was to leave.

Rip said, "Feisty little murderer's mighty pleased about having his own spot. Settlin' down like he's just moved into a house that rivals the palace where them kings and queens of England live."

Once we'd staked out our own individual spots, Boz had me bring those boys in one at a time for questioning. Seated the first feller in front of the marshal's desk and went at him pretty hot and heavy.

Boz got the first question. "What's your name, mister?"

Man looked a bit reluctant to turn loose of any information for a second or so. Rip punched him on the shoulder and said, "Ranger Tatum asked you a question. Cough it up, boy. What's your name?"

Prisoner hung his head and mumbled, "Orvis Tate."

Boz snickered. "Well I'll just be damned. Tell me, Orvis. How'd a west Texas badman like you get all the way over here in the Redlands? Perhaps more important than that, why are you here? I can't imagine why you rode all the way from El Paso just to rob a two-bit bank in Lone Pine."

"You heard of this feller, Boz?" I asked.

"Yeah, heard a story or two about him. Hard to believe the dung heap in front of me is the same killer and thief, though."

Tate looked like Boz'd hurt his feelings. "Ain't no call to be insulting, Ranger."

Rip almost fell off the edge of the desk laughing. Recovered himself and snapped, "What the hell would you know about being insulted? You're under arrest for attempted bank robbery and murder of a town marshal. That last charge could very well turn into real murder if Tuttle dies. Then you're a dead man for sure. The good folks of Lone Pine will put you on trial. Hang you the next day. And you're sittin' here all insulted. Christ Almighty, what's the world comin' to?"

Boz crossed his arms and rested them on top of the desk. "Let's try again. Make it easy this time, Orvis. Why are you here?"

Tate shook his head like a tired dog. "Been down on our luck for a spell. Heard tell a couple of rich ranchers up in Iron Bluff was hirin' guns. Being as we was gettin' pretty hard up, me'n Harold McCormick decided we'd ride over this way. See if 'n we could get some work."

Boz perked up again. "The dead man was Harold McCormick?"

"Yessir. That he was."

My partner shot me a concerned look and said, "Well, I did have some reservations about you cuttin' down on that ole boy when you did it, Lucius. But if he really was McCormick, you probably did all three of us a favor by blasting him when you did. Between the two of 'em, Mr. Tate here ain't nowhere near the badman his friend was."

Rip grinned and said, "Be careful, Boz. You're gettin' insultin' again."

"Who'd you expect to hire on with, Orvis?" I asked.

"Didn't matter to us. We usually go with whoever pays the most. Friend of mine, name of Alvin Clements, rides for Romulus Pitt. But I didn't care one way or t'other. Just needed some coin comin' my way."

Boz kicked back in his chair, ran sweaty fingers through his hair, and moaned. "Just keeps gettin' worse. Alvin Clements is a real bloodcurdling story from down near Cuero. Got started on the owlhoot trail by killing his parents and grandparents the same day. Been murderin' folks by the wagon load ever since."

Rip said, "You keep some pretty sorry company, Orvis. Kind of men who can get you killed, or hung, real easy. But I suppose you already knew that."

"Either of the families, Tingwell or Pitt, aware you were on the way?" I asked.

"Both of 'em. Planned on somethin' like a biddin' war for our services when we arrived. Just stopped here long enough to get a little travelin' money. Way our luck's been runnin', though, don't surprise me much that you bastards interrupted a perfectly good bank robbery, and kilt poor Harold. Figure a hangin' has to be the next stop in my cowshit future."

Boz motioned for me to take our prisoner back to his cell. As Tate stood, my friend said, "You're real close, Orvis. Tuttle passes on to the Great Beyond and you'll swing sure as Pontius Pilate's stoking fires in the bowels of hell."

We brought Tate's only living running buddy, Gaston Perkins, out and talked with him as well. But he didn't have much to add to the tale we'd already heard.

Spent the last few hours before dark visiting with citizens, shopkeepers, bartenders, and such. Asked a few inoffensive questions, but decided to wait a day or so before really bearing down on anyone. Me and Boz figured it might be a good idea to kind of ingratiate ourselves with the locals before saying anything that might turn them against us.

Found a right nice cafe in the six-room Excelsior Hotel. Place named Mae's. Spirited Irish lady, Molly Mae Mitchell, ran it. Woman could do wonders with a piece of beefsteak. For reasons beyond my understanding, she took an instant liking to Boz. Actually more than a liking. Woman was at least fifteen years younger than my partner, a damn sight better-looking, and still had the freckle-faced appearance of a girl. Hard not to notice how she rubbed up against ole Boz when serving our food, or how the brown-eyed lady couldn't seem to get enough of his company anytime she came to our table.

Even Rip spotted it. "Think she's yours for the takin', Boz. Woman can barely keep herself under control. Yes, indeedy. Miss Molly Mae's about as antsy as it gets. Way I hear it, her dearly de-parted husband has been de-parted for more'n a year now. You don't watch yourself, old friend, she's gonna land in your pants like a pair of store-bought drawers."

Boz acted embarrassed, and shamed, all to hell and gone. Found out a few days later, he'd been sneaking over to visit with the affectionate lady anytime he could steal a few minutes away from us.

Townsfolk warmed up right quick like. Tuttle managed to stay alive, but didn't look to be good for much of anything for at least six months or so. Citizens appeared mighty thankful a jailhouse full of heavily armed Rangers had presented themselves. Guess they felt safer having us around. That is, till the day Romulus Pitt showed up.

We'd barely got breakfast to the prisoners and fed ourselves when Rip said, "You hear that? Horses comin'. Lots of 'em."

Ominous rumble from north of town thundered our

direction; then rolled up and rattled the front door like some monstrous, growling animal.

Must have been a dozen horsed men milling around for a minute or so before we heard someone yell, "You Rangers get out here. We've got palavering to do." Considerable belligerence couched in those instructions.

Rip stayed inside with his shotgun at the ready. Me and Boz armed ourselves with everything we had. By the time we hit the boardwalk, I was carrying damned near anything that'd shoot, stab, or beat the hell out of anyone or anything as the situation presented itself.

All those horses had finally calmed a bit, and most of the nervous movement stopped. Boz eased up to the edge of the walk not more than two or three steps from our pack of visitors. I signaled Rip of my intentions, then crawfished to a spot where I could get a better view of what appeared destined to cook up into an extremely volatile situation. Way we'd spread out, at least one of us could see damn near whatever those riders might try.

Boz surveyed the testy-looking crew and said, "Well, we're here. You gonna say something or just sit on your lathered-up animals and sweat?"

Man who appeared about the way you'd figure God must look on a good day snatched his slouch hat off. He wiped the saturated band, and his flowing mane of white hair, with a bandanna the size of a pillow slip. Didn't look at us at first. Stared at the inside of the well-used head cover while he talked.

"Name's Romulus Pitt, gents. All these men ride for me. Hear tell you strolled into town and, in a matter of minutes, managed to save the bank, Marshal Tuttle, and several mistreated citizens. Mighty fine day's work."

Boz said, "We do appreciate the compliment, sir. Feel it's our job to help out when we can."

"Did you know those boys you've got in your lockup work for me?"

"Not according to Orvis Tate. He says they'd not decided on an employer. Wanted to test the waters and see who'd come up with the most money." Boz looked pleased when the old man glanced up and glared back at him.

Just to remind the belligerent bunch my partner wasn't alone, I said, "They're gonna be employed by the state of Texas after their trials. Be breaking rocks down at the state penitentiary for a spell, I imagine."

Pitt slapped the battered hat back on his head. "Also hear tell you've been asking discreet questions about me and my family." Old bastard sneered like he'd just sucked on a less-than-ripe persimmon.

"Could be," Boz said.

"Well, I rode over from Iron Bluff this morning to tell you that me and my sons, here on either side of me, don't appreciate it one damned bit. We want it stopped."

Not much difficulty telling which of the Pitt bunch his sons were. They looked like younger versions of the old man. Almost like twins. Except that one of them was blond and clean-shaven—the other just a bit darker and sporting a handlebar mustache. Figured the dark one was Eli. He appeared a little older and had a meaner look around the eyes.

Saw Boz's upper lip peel back from his teeth like a dog about to take a plug out of an offensive hand near his food. He snarled, "Well, sir, I don't personally give a good goddamn what you want. We're Texas Rangers on the business of the state and will ask whatever questions, seek out anyone we decide to speak with, go where we want, and do anything necessary to get the information we require. Far as me and my partners are concerned, you Pitts can take your wants and go straight to hell with them."

Romulus Pitt was obviously not accustomed to having anyone speak to him in such a manner. In spite of the morning heat, you could see the color rise from the collar of his shirt. Thought his ears would burst into flame right before my very eyes. Same reaction was duplicated on the faces of the whelps at his side.

Got to admit, though, he kept himself under control as he turned in the saddle and said, "Perhaps you should meet one of my men, Ranger." He motioned to someone behind him I couldn't see. A man, dressed in black from head to foot, urged a long-legged stallion the same color to a spot between Pitt and one of his sons. He reined up, leaned forward on his saddle horn, and put on quite a display of arrogant insolence. Pistoleer packed a pair of bone-handled Colts mounted high on his waist and backward in the Hickok style.

Pitt made an offhanded motion toward his gunman and snapped, "This here's Nick Fox. You might've heard of him."

Boz turned slightly sideways to the group and leveled his shotgun on Pitt. Appeared to me, if he dropped a hammer on the man, he'd get Fox too. Already had mine on the dark-haired son, and some of his cohorts on the old man's right side. Figured Rip had those on the left all measured up for a coffin as well.

Fox straightened when he saw Boz's move. Barrels of that coach gun must have looked as big a pair of Mexican sombreros. He said, "Me'n Boz have already met, Mr. Pitt." It came out kind of strangled. Like he had a cocklebur stuck in his craw. "How you doin' these days, Boz?"

"Just fine, Nick. Been killing any children lately? Had an opportunity to run down any old ladies in the streets this morning?"

Angry frown creased the gunman's forehead. He snorted, "Careful, Boz. You're right on the edge of stepping in places I don't let most men go."

Got to admit, when it came to a face-down, Ranger Boz Tatum was a man you wanted on your side. Completely fearless. He didn't even hesitate when he came back all friendly like with, "Well, Nick my boy, wouldn't want to stay on the wrong side of a treacherous edge. Think I'll just jump over with both feet. Have you told your employer here how such a dangerous reputation has managed to attach itself to your evil hide?"

Man in black snarled, "Done told you, Tatum, you're steppin' onto treacherous ground."

Boz thumbed the hammers on the shotgun. Even those in back of the Pitt party came to attention when they snapped. He kept talking like he hadn't heard a word Fox said. "Mr. Pitt, you might be interested in this tale. 'Bout six years ago, your employee here started his life of crime by attempting to rob a bank in the south Texas town of Agua Caliente. Had about the same amount of luck as them boys we jailed yesterday. Got no money, but ran a poor woman down in the street when he attempted to get away. Killed her. Spent three years in prison for involuntary manslaughter."

Fox's right hand moved, ever so slightly, toward his pistol. Boz said, "You touch that gun, Nick, and you'll force me to send for Mr. Melton, the town undertaker. He'll have to dig graves for you and two or three others on either side of you." Fox looked flustered, and slowly placed the hand back on his saddle horn.

Boz brightened up and continued his tale almost like he was telling a favorite joke. "Well, ever since Agua Caliente, Nick's gone and killed more'n a dozen people. At least that's the widely held belief. Law hasn't been able to definitely prove any of them—yet. Truth is, Mr. Pitt, your man's something of a sneak. Personally don't believe he's got nerve enough to do any killing in the light, and facing his intended victim. So if you came here this morning on a mission designed to intimidate the Texas Rangers with a back-shooting weasel, you'd best give your tactics a little more thought."

Ole Man Pitt looked downright chastised for about a second. Then he roared, "You bastards do as you wish here in Lone Pine, but stay away from Iron Bluff. You come to my town and there'll be hell to pay. And I'll be the one collecting."

He started to back his horse away. As he did, Boz shouted, "We come and go as we please, Mr. Pitt. Inform your town marshal he can expect a visit no later than day after tomorrow. We're here to prevent what looks like coming warfare. Believe me when I tell you, sir, we'll do whatever it takes."

The blond kid stood in his stirrups and hocked a nasty gob of spittle at Boz. Big wad of stuff landed on the step just below Boz's feet. Then all three of the Pitts twirled their mounts in tight circles and galloped back the way they'd come. Rest of the gang followed. All but Fox. He made a show of slowly backing his tall black horse away in a kind of gunman's retreat. Soon as he turned the animal and kicked for Iron Bluff, Boz blew out a long-winded sigh and eased the hammers down of his shotgun. Slumped at the shoulders like he'd been chopping wood all day.

He forced a sheepish grin and muttered, "Damn, that was close."

Rip jerked the jail door open and said, "I thought you said that Fox feller was a bad 'un."

Boz fell into one of the chairs on the boardwalk. "He is. Real bad. Just as bad as his reputation. But I'd bet my next month's pay, most of them he's killed died in the dark and had holes in their backs. Sometimes if you challenge a killer like Fox with the truth, it rattles him right down to the ground. Merely took a chance, Rip. Seems to have worked."

I flopped into the battered seat beside Boz. Stretched my legs out and rolled a smoke. Not a sound from the town. No dogs barking, no chickens clucking, no kids running around, nothing.

I said, "Damn, it's quiet. Almost like we're the only living souls within a hundred miles, ain't it?"

Boz glanced from one end of the street to the other. "Folks are scared. They realize we've stirred up a hornet's nest and are afraid they might get stung. Bet it's gonna be hard to pry anything useful out of them from now on. Wish we'd asked a few questions about Wag's niece before Pitt and his gang of cutthroats blew into town. Just didn't think of it."

I wanted to make him feel a little better. "Forgot to tell you 'bout it, but yesterday at the café I talked with a lady named Neeva Skaggs who remembered the day Ruby Black passed through town. She told me the girl got off the westbound stage when it stopped so passengers could have a bite to eat at Mae's place."

"Mae Mitchell saw Ruby?"

"Must have. Mrs. Skaggs said the girl was there for at least an hour. If she's as much a looker as Wag claimed, I don't see how Mae could have missed her."

We left Rip with the prisoners and hoofed it over to the Excelsior as quick as we could. Desk clerk was the only person I saw in the hotel lobby. No customers at all in Mae's place. Followed Boz as he strolled through the dining room and into the kitchen. Cookstove compounded the already stifling heat in the place. Smell of baking pies wafted up and tickled my nose with cinnamon, sugar, and bubbling apples. Mrs. Mitchell sat at a table near the only window in the room. I couldn't spot a drop of sweat on the lady. Amazing.

Boz removed his hat and said, "Mornin', Mrs. Mitchell. Could we have a word with you?"

The smile that greeted us began to fade as she realized Boz's unexpected appearance didn't involve a social call. She said, "Of course you can, Ranger Tatum." I felt certain her forced reserve was for my benefit.

Boz glanced through the window and said, "How 'bout we go outside and sit on your bench there in the shade. Might not be much cooler, but it's hotter'n hell's front doorknob in here."

He escorted Mrs. Mitchell to the coarse brush arbor some sixty feet behind the hotel. She seated herself on a crude loveseat. Primly smoothed her apron-covered dress with both hands, and waited. Shriveling leaves from distressed vines covered the unpainted latticework overhead.

Thought Boz would sit next to his new lady friend, but he didn't. We stood with our hats in our hands as he said, "Want you to cast your memory back a spell, ma'am. More'n a month ago. Young lady named Ruby Black got off the westbound stage and had a meal in your café. Well-dressed, in her early twenties, reddest hair you've probably ever seen. Blue eyes. A real clock-stopper that every man around would have noticed. Hope you can recall her."

Lady brightened up immediately. "Of course I remember her. A real beauty. Not just physically either. Most pleasant young woman I've had in my place in a long while. Gracious and extremely well-mannered."

"Did she say anything unusual you might bring to mind?" I asked.

"No, nothing unusual." She stopped, lapsed into thought for a second, and said, "But I did find her choice of male company a bit odd."

Boz perked up. "What do you mean by odd, Mae?"

"Well, she came in on the arm of Morgan Tingwell. Not

what I'd call the most desirable of escorts for a young woman of her obvious quality. If I remember correctly, they weren't what you'd call an item, but had simply kept company on the same stage all the way from New Orleans."

I jumped at that one. "Did Tingwell say or do anything you remember?"

Mrs. Mitchell scratched her head and looked pensive for a moment before she answered. "Young man didn't talk much. He appeared absolutely smitten with the girl, though. Couldn't take his eyes off her. Overly protective, I thought. Morgan got testy when other men made it a point to stop at their table to supposedly speak with him, but smiled and tipped their hats to the girl. His behavior made patrons sitting near them a bit uncomfortable. I recall that Neeva Skaggs and her husband got so uneasy they left before finishing their meal. Not like Otto Skaggs at all."

"Did you notice any tension between the young couple, other than the Tingwell boy's petulance at having other men notice and acknowledge Miss Black?" I heard a more pronounced concern in Boz's voice when he asked that question.

"No. But I must admit she made little, if any, attempt to return his obvious efforts at flirtation. She merely seemed like a courteous young woman having a bit of fun at the expense of an overly amorous young man. Not sure he possessed enough in the way of worldliness to understand exactly what was going on."

Sounded like we'd pretty much wrung that rag out. I said, "Did she leave on the stage?"

"Couldn't say. I have to assume so. They left the café together. I've not seen either of them since that night. Course Morgan Tingwell doesn't get down this direction very often anyway. Only reason I recognized him was because a friend pointed the boy out on one of my visits to Iron Bluff.

His family is well known there—especially his brother Hardy. Folks up that way have developed something along the lines of morbid fear when it comes to Hardy. Many say he's a dangerous man to get crosswise of."

We thanked Mrs. Mitchell for all the information. Boz kind of motioned me away. I made my excuses, and headed back to the jail. He stayed for almost an hour longer. Don't think he got much in the way of additional enlightenment on the subject.

Didn't matter anyway. Soon as he walked in the door of the jail, he said, "Well, boys, looks like we're gonna have to get over to Iron Bluff and visit the Tingwell family tomorrow. Hoped we could put it off till everything settled down a bit, but I want to talk to Morgan as soon as possible."

"What about the prisoners?" Rip asked.

"I've made arrangements for Mrs. Mitchell to feed them twice a day. Any problems at the jail and she's to send word to us as quickly as possible."

"Really think that'll work, Boz?" I asked.

"Should," he said. "Near as I can tell, it's only ten miles to Iron Bluff. The Tingwell ranch is about five miles on the other side of town."

Rip chuckled, then said, "Personally, I don't really give a damn if poor luck should befall these snakes."

Boz kept going like he hadn't even heard Rip's comment. "Good rider should be able to find us in less than two hours no matter what happens. Besides, I've already warned these bastards of the consequences if they try to get away. Don't think Toefield would leave his cell even if we opened the door and told him he could go."

"Sounds good. When do we leave?" I asked.

"Tomorrow morning. We'll try to time it so we catch them at their noon meal. Always puts folks into a lather if you show up unexpected when they're about to eat. I want to throw a real surprise into this Tingwell bunch. Get a good night's sleep. We'll go in armed to the teeth and lookin' meaner'n hell."

5

"Meanest Sons of Bitches I Done Ever Run up Against"

IRON BLUFF LOOKED enough like Lone Pine to make them almost indistinguishable from one another. Have to admit, though, the bustling village did seem busier. Lot more by way of foot traffic in and around the local stores and shops.

Town marshal resided in what appeared a much nicer combination living quarters and jail than Lone Pine's. Whole shebang was a fine-looking red-stone building. Stood right next to a watering hole named the Fin and Feather. Saloon's façade was painted forest green trimmed in red. Heavy, double-thick glass window sported the name in fancy gold-leaf lettering. Looked more like an Austin gentlemen's club than a saloon. Discreetly tucked in a lower corner of the pane, in much smaller script, you could read ROMULUS PITT-OWNER.

Directly across the street squatted a second liquor emporium of considerably lesser size and elegance. The

Matador didn't look to have ever been touched by a paint-brush. Sign in front was fashioned from a rough plank by an unknown person of little ability who'd burned the name in with a branding iron. Several flea-bitten dogs lounged on the boardwalk in front of the place, and a number of rough-looking cowboys occupied chairs propped against the wall. Several of the waddies whittled at pine pickets and watched our every move as we passed.

I had suggested earlier that we ride around the town to try and keep from stirring anything up, but Boz wouldn't hear of it. He snapped, "Hell with these sons of bitches. If Ole Man Pitt's badge-carryin' bulldog, or any of these other brush-poppers, wants part of me, just let him say the wrong thing. Ain't a city marshal or leather-burner in Texas gonna tell Rangers where to go or how to conduct our business. We're here on assignment from the com-manding officer of Company B and can do whatever the hell's necessary, as far as we can see it." Thus ended that conversation.

Ambled through the settlement loaded for bear and looking like a tiny army of the extremely pissed off. Boz didn't even try to avoid Pitt's version of the law. Rode right up to the front door of the man's office and called him out. Tall, nice-looking gent sporting a handlebar mustache and iron-gray hair came to the door. He wiped shaving soap from his face and neck with a much-used towel. Didn't hesitate or look the least bit intimidated.

Iron Bluff's marshal stepped up to the edge of his porch and said, "Do something for you fellers?" About then, I guess, he realized who we were. "Oh, you're the Rangers Mr. Pitt said might be stopping in. Why don't you boys climb down and come inside. I got a fresh pot of coffee from the Fin and Feather just a few minutes ago."

Boz threw me a quick glance and winked. Then turned

back to Iron Bluff's lawman. "Name's Boz Tatum. Heavily armed feller on my right is Lucius Dodge. This 'un here is Rip Thorn. Stopped by to let you know we'll be prowlin' around these parts until such time as several problems that are of interest to our superiors are resolved. Wondered if you had any problem with that, Marshal . . . uh-h-h . . . sorry I didn't get your name."

"Bronson Stonehill. Pleased to make your acquaintance Ranger Tatum, Dodge, Thorn. And no, I don't have any problem with investigations you might need to conduct while visiting in my jurisdiction. See no reason you shouldn't do as you deem fit."

He sounded reasonable enough to me. So I took it on myself and said, "We do appreciate it, Marshal Stonehill."

Think I might have been a bit premature in my assessment. Soon as the words got out of my mouth, he draped the towel over his shoulder and said, "Long as you keep me informed of all your actions beforehand." He put particular emphasis on the word beforehand.

Boz didn't miss a beat. "Can't guarantee anything even vaguely resembling such a request, sir. We tend to move about at our own leisure, and don't feel compelled to inform anyone of our intentions. Think you'd agree that sometimes such courtesies aren't possible."

Stonehill kind of swelled up. Put his hands on his hips and frowned. "Don't think you understand, Ranger Tatum. I'm not *requesting* anything. I'm telling you that's the way it's gotta be, if you want to function around my town."

Rip and I both glanced at Boz. Don't know about Rip, but I could tell our friend was spoiling for a fight, and teetered right on the verge of jumping off his horse and kicking the stump juice out of Iron Bluff's smart-mouthed law-enforcement officer. Muscles in his jaw tightened up. Squint got so tight I couldn't see his eyes.

Still and all, Boz maintained what sounded like an even temper and said, "As I understand it, you're Iron Bluff's *town* marshal. Ain't that so, Mr. Stonehill?"

Freshly shaved gent looked confused for a second or so before he said, "Yes. That's correct."

"Well, I hate to be the one to inform you of this, ole son, but your jurisdiction ends at the town limits. Ours covers the entire state of Texas and any goddamned where else we feel compelled to go. So don't be making demands on us that you have no legal backing for."

Stonehill's face reddened. He blinked real fast, several times, and his right hand dropped to a spot on his hip where a pistol should have resided. Big artery on the side of his neck bulged out. Honest-to-God, you could see the blood pulsing through it. Thought for a minute his head might explode.

After ten or fifteen seconds of hard staring, he said, "Mr. Pitt warned me you would be trouble, Tatum. Mentioned you were pretty full of yourself. I can see now he didn't miss the mark much in that assessment."

"Well, that's a gunnysack full of horseshit, sir. I'm simply a man with a job to do. Long as you stay out of my way—and don't try to get quarrelsome with me—we'll get along just fine. Came by this morning to let you know we're on our way out to the Tingwell ranch to speak with one of the sons. Young feller named Morgan."

"I'd be careful of that bunch, Mr. Tatum. Especially since a newly hired gunhand was brought in to run with John Roman Hatch. His name's Casper Longstreet. He can be deadly." Stonehill smiled like he took great pleasure in telling us the bad news.

Rip perked up and asked, "What's this Longstreet feller look like, Marshal?"

Stonehill threw his head back and laughed. Then he said,

"If you meet a feller that looks like he died about a week ago, you will have found him. Might as well get yourselves prepared. Ain't gonna be a pleasant sight. No, gents, it sure as hell ain't."

Iron Bluff's marshal turned and started back for his door, but stopped and faced us again as if he'd forgotten something. "If you don't run into him at the ranch, just come on back to town and visit the Matador. Sit around a spell. Cut the dust with a few drinks. Sooner or later, Casper will show up. Have a pleasant trip, Rangers. Say hello to Hatch and Longstreet for me when you meet them." We could hear him indulging in a fit of derisive laughter once he got back inside his jail.

Didn't have any trouble finding the Tingwell place. Only had to ask one old-timer for directions. He'd staked out a shady spot under a live oak near the center of town. Site sheltered the geezer from a blazing sun that bored holes in high gauzy clouds like bullets going through bedsheets.

Boz asked which way we needed to go. Ancient codger lifted a withered arm and said, around the stem of his corn-cob pipe, "Jist foller this here road on north, young feller. You'll come on a split 'bout five or eight mile outside town. One branch goes east to the Pitt ranch, t'other heads west for the Tingwells' spread. Signs on each path make it right clear where you'll end up. Course, they's also pert clear you ain't wanted. Personally feel it'd be in yore best interest to stay clear."

Rip leaned down and handed the old man a maduro panatela by way of thanks. Codger saluted us with the cigar by tapping the brim of his hat. Rip said, "They really that unfriendly, pops?"

Our guide gave his ragged beard a sagelike scratch. "Well, sonny, next month'll be my eighty-seventh birthday, near as I can figure. Been around the tree once or twice.

Fought in the big war. Attended a rodeo or two. Even traveled to New-goddamned-York. Seen The Naked Lady herself, Adah Isaacs Menken, ride on stage unclothed in *Mazeppa.* Thought I knowed, or had met, all kinds. But them Tingwells is about the meanest sons of bitches I done ever run up against. Even their women are a sight. Wouldn't touch one of them dirty-legged females with a stick of firewood. Careful out there, boys. Ain't nobody safe around that bunch."

We followed the antique gomer's directions exactly. Less than an hour later, we reined up outside a heavy wooden gate that bore all the earmarks of having been constructed by someone who had less knowledge of carpentry than a flying squirrel.

Rip got down and shoved it open. As we passed through he said, "The house don't look too bad from here, but if this piece of woodworking is any indication of what lies ahead, I hate to imagine what these folk must live in."

Sweet Jesus, but the Tingwell dwelling turned out worse than we could have imagined. As we made our way across the two hundred yards of rolling pastureland between the fence and their rough residence, Boz said, "Looks like they picked up driftwood from the river and just stacked it up, willy-nilly, for the past decade."

Rip grunted his agreement, then added, "Resembles a gigantic pile of deer antlers with a stovepipe stickin' out of the roof, don't it? My God, it's huge. Bet this place has more'n a dozen rooms."

All along the fence line, which ran on either side of the rough road from the monstrous gate to the house, laid an astonishing collection of trash. Wagon parts, pieces of old harness, stacks of paper tied in rotting twine, rusted farm implements of every imaginable kind, pieces of a busted-up Butterfield stagecoach, pots, pans, and even broken tableware rested amidst weeds three feet high. Some of the stuff seemed to be arranged in stacks to resemble the shapes of men and imaginary creatures.

Boz muttered, "You ever seen anything to match this?"

Shook my head and said, "Not me."

We'd barely pulled our mounts to a stop in front of the place when the plank door popped open. Four armed men jumped into the dusty, chicken-filled yard, and spread out in a single line. Pullets squawked and ran in every direction.

Boz got his wish. We had even surprised their pack of mangy ill-fed dogs. Must have been a dozen of them sleeping beneath what resembled a porch, until the racket generated by all those folks flying out of their nightmarish house woke them up. Set off a hellacious racket of howling, barking, and snapping that went on till one of the men kicked and prodded the pack back to their filthy den.

Line of bodies parted, and a stocky-built, square-headed elderly man pushed his way to the front. He dressed himself in red wool pants, green shirt, and a bright yellow beaver top hat that must have been forty years old.

He stood in front of his angry family with his fists on his hips and yelped, "Did you ill-mannered bastards not see the signs on the road warnin' unwanted folk to keep out? This here is private property. We don't be entertainin' no visitors."

Boz leaned slightly forward and crossed his arms on the horn of his saddle. "We saw your signs, Mr. Tingwell. Such advice doesn't apply to us."

The elder Tingwell torqued his head to one side, bugged an unblinking eye at us, and snapped, "Is that a natural-born fact, my bucko. And who do you think you are to ignore such warnings, and then be bold enough to tell me you don't have to be a-payin' heed to our warnin's? Think you're Sam Houston, or some other such Texican royalty?"

I edged Grizz a step closer and stopped him right beside Boz. Said, "No, sir, but we're close enough."

"Damned if you are," Tingwell snapped.

Boz held a calming hand my direction. "My impetuous young friend's way of trying to tell you we're Texas Rangers here on official business."

Kid missing several teeth in front sidled up next to the old man and slobbered, "We 'uns don't be givin' a tinker's damn 'bout no goddamned Rangers—Texas or otherwise. Turn them animals around and head back the way you come."

Guess Boz held no desire to debate the question of our authority. His voice dropped to the cold-as-a-well-rope-in-Montana level when he said, "Best tell your family to put their guns away, sir. If your firearms ain't outta my face in exactly one minute, there'll be so many dead Tingwells in front of this rat's nest, it'll take somebody a week to bury all of 'em."

Different one of the boys said, "Let's jist shoot the hell out of 'em, Pap. We'll bury 'em in the river."

Old man snapped back with, "Shut yer mouth, Morgan. Don't think this man is bluffin'." So, there it was. Hardy had to be the one missing his teeth. No wonder people feared the boy. He appeared possessed of a mean streak that probably went all the way to the bone.

While not near as repulsive, or as much of a dental oddity as his brother, Morgan wouldn't have been considered anything like a catch for the loneliest spinster north of the Rio Grande. I couldn't imagine a woman of Ruby Black's description having anything to do with him. You could've raised a crop of corn under his fingernails.

The Tingwell family's leader was having second thoughts. Worry lines creased his forehead, and a river of sweat poured from under his ancient hat.

Boz bored in on him. "Trust my words on this matter, sir. You aren't ready for the kind of gunfight about to occur here if you don't do exactly as I say. Even if we lose, an entire company of Rangers will show up within a few weeks, wipe out what's left of your clan, and erase this place from the face of the earth. You've got fifteen seconds."

Pap Tingwell thought it over for about another second and barked, "Put yer guns away, boys. We'll talk with these bastards and see what they's about."

Some confusion prevailed for a spell. Pap got right irritated with the brood's inability to carry out his shouted wishes. Considerable yelling and swearing prevailed until they had all disarmed. He sent most of the litter back inside, but kept his two remaining sons with him.

Once the arsenal had finally disappeared, and things had calmed down a bit, the old man said, "There you are, Ranger. Satisfied is yah?"

Boz motioned us down, and we climbed off our animals. He walked straight up to Bull Tingwell. Handed the old man and both the sons a cigar. They looked shocked to their boot soles for a few seconds. Once everyone got lit up and puffing, the situation loosened up dramatically.

Pap took a deep drag on what was probably the best tobacco he had smoked in years and puffed gunmetal gray rings at the sky. As they floated away he said, "Official business, is it? What kind of official business would you law-bringers be havin' with the likes of us?"

Boz turned to me and said, "Tell him why we're here, Lucius."

"We're looking for a missing girl, Mr. Tingwell. Her name is Ruby Black. Red hair, blue eyes, extremely beautiful young woman. Well educated. Trained for the teaching profession."

Tingwell almost choked on his smoke. Both of his boys

got real twitchy. Snaggle-toothed one, that I figured had to be Hardy, threw his head back, sneered, and said, "Why would you think we'd know anything about such a woman?"

Rip hadn't said much all day. He surprised us when he boomed out, "Because your brother, Morgan here, was the last person to be seen with her." All three Tingwell heads snapped Rip's direction. The way they reacted, you'd have thought he dropped a diamondbacked rattler in their pants.

The old man tried to cover it up. "Well, sorry to say we can't be a-helpin' ye, Rangers. Cain't say as how my son done seen that woman since the stage dropped him off in Iron Bluff."

Morgan looked like a weasel with its foot caught in a steel trap. I pressed the issue. "That a fact, Morgan? You've not seen Miss Black since the time your father just described?"

Man barely found the ability to breathe, "No. No. I ain't seen that gal since."

We knew he was lying. Hell, all of them had lied. All of a sudden, the old man got hot again. "Yep, there's the problem. You badge-wearin' bastards work for Pitt, don't you. This is nothin' more'n a ruse to get us off the land so's he can take it from us. Well, by Godfrey, it ain't a-gonna be workin'. No, by God, not for a second it ain't."

Rip snorted, "Jesus, old man, are you crazier than a shithouse rat on top of everything else? We don't work for Pitt any more than you do."

Hardy spit all over himself when he yelled, "You asskissers go back to Pitt and tell him he's got a killin' comin', and damned soon. We're gonna have our revenge for them rubbin' Buster out. Sure as tamales make farts."

"We thought maybe Albert Pitt's death paid that debt off," Boz said.

The Tingwells all shouted simultaneously, "We didn't kill Albert Pitt."

Bull Tingwell seethed like a man about to explode. "Dumb bastard must've fell off his horse and drowned. His corpse didn't have a mark on it made by my family." Tobacco juice dribbled from the corner of his mouth and dropped onto his puke green shirt. Rest of the group got agitated again as he shouted, "But by God, the next time we meet them bastards they's gonna be killings. It's a gar-un-teed lock-nutted cinch."

Boz couldn't let that one pass. "Careful, old man. You're about to let your mouth get ahead of your brain."

"Not likely, Ranger. I done got us two men ain't afraid of the Pitts, God, Texas Rangers, nor anything else living. Figure if Pitt can have two killers walking the streets of Iron Bluff, so can I. You're damned lucky John Roman Hatch and Casper Longstreet ain't here this fine mornin'. You'd be dead as Julius Caesar by now."

Boz turned to me. "We're not gettin' anywhere here. Let's saddle up and give Mr. Tingwell and his family time to talk all this over for a spell. We'll come back again later. There's time a-plenty." Then he turned to ole Bull again, smiled, and said, "We'll be back, Mr. Tingwell. Soon."

Left them standing there jabbering and yelling like wild people. Once we'd passed through their gate Rip said, "You fellers did notice how they reacted to questions about the girl, didn't you?"

"Yeah, we saw it, Rip," I said, "They're hiding something. Wouldn't surprise me a bit if Miss Ruby Black ain't locked up somewhere in that dreadful house of theirs. You think we can get a court order and search the place, Boz?"

Boz reined up and gave the problem some thought for a few seconds. "Normally I wouldn't even bother. But we've got a touchy situation at hand here. They'll probably fight if we just try to march in."

"What about the court order?" I said again.

"Pretty certain we're not gonna get one around here. But we just might find a friendly judge willing to help us out in Shelbyville. Rip, I want you to burn leather that way. See if you can get an audience with Judge Stanley Cooper. Tell him I sent you and what's going on here. Pretty certain he'll send you back with exactly what we need. Shouldn't take but two or three days at most. Best get moving right now. No need wastin' time."

Rip didn't hesitate. Yelled over his shoulder as he whipped his animal away from us, "I'll be back quick as I can."

Boz pulled his hat off, and wiped his face with a wet bandanna. "You know, Lucius, we're sitting on a powder keg that has at least a dozen fuses runnin' to it." He looked tired when he said, "God above, I hope we make it out of this one alive. Keep 'em loaded and close at hand. I think things are about to really heat up around Iron Bluff."

I said, "Damn, Boz it's scorching enough for me right now."

"I know. But once the killing gets started, our situation's gonna get hotter by a damn sight—as blisterin' as forty acres of Satan's playground."

6

"FELT COMPELLED TO KILL
HIM AFORE HE KILT ME"

TOOK OUR TIME getting back to town. Boz tended to think better in the saddle. So we just kind of ambled along while he mulled the situation over. Got back to Iron Bluff and had barely tied our animals to the hitch rack in front of the jail when all hell broke loose.

A man dressed in a white shirt, sleeve garters, and apron of a shopkeeper hoofed it up to us and said, "Gentlemen, my name is Breedlove. Horace Breedlove. Own the mercantile across the street, there on the other side of the Matador."

We tipped our hats and said, "Howdy."

Breedlove didn't stop. Pointed to the Matador and said, "Casper Longstreet came in this morning just after eleven o'clock. Customers have told me he's bragging as how he intends to kill someone from the Pitt clan before the day is out. Fin and Feather filled up with Pitt riders 'bout half an hour ago. Didn't take long for them to hear about Longstreet's threat."

Held my hand up to slow Horace down. Man talked so fast I had trouble understanding him at times. "Been any trouble yet, Mr. Breedlove?" I asked.

He nervously fingered the hem of his apron. "No. Not so far. But both camps have been drinking for a couple of hours. Trouble's coming. You can feel it. There's blood in the air."

"Where's Marshal Stonehill?"

Breedlove got even more nervous when I asked that question. "Have no idea, Ranger. But it ain't uncommon for him to disappear anytime one of the Tingwells' pair of gunfighters shows up in town. Fact is, he almost always has 'business' somewhere else if anything threatening occurs. Ole Man Pitt may own the marshal, but Stonehill looks out for himself. Sorry state of affairs for the good people of Iron Bluff when they can't trust the town's keeper of the peace to protect them."

Boz scratched his chin and looked thoughtful. I could hear the tough whiskers rasp against the ends of calloused fingers. "Well," he said, "Lucius and I'll stroll over to the Matador and have a talk with Mr. Longstreet. See if we can't snuff this out before something wayward occurs."

"You sure about that, Boz?"

"Yeah, Lucius. Knew a nose-to-nose dustup like this was coming sooner or later. Might as well put a stopper in it now. Get your shotgun. Stay behind me. Cover my back. I'll talk to Longstreet."

Never have liked walking into potential gunfire. I'd managed to survive flying lead on numerous occasions, including scores of fights with Comanche raiders, and killed my share of those who'd stepped over the line. Didn't have a bit of trouble rubbing out anyone who threatened me—or mine. Especially belly-slinking, bank-robbing snakes like Harold McCormick and his ilk.

Men of Longstreet's breed were a totally different bucket of worms. They tended to be calculating, deadly, and often unpredictable. Scores of the unsuspecting had died at the hands of such men for any real, or perceived, provocation, and prosecution was almost impossible. Juries in Texas rarely convicted anyone who entered a plea of self-defense.

Scratching your nose at the wrong time could get a man killed. The defendant would swear before God, and the law, that, "Well, I thought sure enough he was a-reachin' and a-grabbin' fer his hog leg. Only defendin' myself when I wuz forced to shoot the poor bastard eight times with three different guns, Your Honor."

And when the already beaten prosecutor asked, "Did you ever think he might have simply had an itchy nose?" the answer would inevitably be, "Looked like he meant to draw down on me when his hand dropped to his side. Felt compelled to kill him afore he kilt me."

Murderers usually always ended up back on the streets, where they invariably managed to kill someone else within a short time. Then the whole process stared over again with the same appalling outcome. Lot of good Texas folk suffered because their juries were so gutless.

I did as instructed. Followed Boz through the coarse saloon's batwing doors. He stopped just inside to let his eyes adjust to the darker interior. Bar ran along the entire wall on our right and matched the rough exterior. No highly polished mahogany, nothing but planks sitting on top of empty beer barrels. Found it somewhat amazing that the mirror behind the makeshift serving top was a heavy, opulent, oddly shaped piece of glass mounted in an expensive and ornate frame. Appeared to be worth more than the rest of the entire cow-country oasis. Rough-cut board floor had never seen a wood plane, or even a broom, from what I could detect.

No doubt where Casper Longstreet had chosen to sit. All the tables used for poker, dominoes, and such lined the left side of the narrow, oblong room. Three in back were empty but for a single man seated as far from the door as he could get. Almost missed seeing him because he'd pushed his chair into the back corner. Heavy cloud of cigar smoke, mixed with the smells of liquor, full spittoons, and sweat, cooked in the stifling heat and created an eye-watering stench that almost brought me to my knees.

Without hesitation, Boz marched right to Longstreet. I heard the hammers come back on his shotgun, so I cocked mine as well. He didn't slow his long-legged stride till his legs brushed against a chair at the gunman's table.

Longstreet sat with a wide-brimmed straw hat pulled down over his face as though he'd dozed off. He didn't bother to look up until Boz bumped the table with the barrel of the shotgun.

Near as I could tell, the description Marshal Stonehill provided us bordered on the amazingly charitable. Casper Longstreet didn't simply look like a dead man; he looked like a dead man that'd been under ground for about a week and then dug up. His was the kind of face Christian mothers scared their unruly children with in order to enforce behavior when all else failed. Pale as a winter moon. Covered with deep pockmarks. A bad dream come to life.

The corpselike gunfighter slowly removed a hat that appeared sloppily vented with a pocket knife. A spiderweb of thin, white hair lay limply on his ghostly pate like sewing thread draped over a child's coffin.

In a voice that sounded as though it came from a throat seriously damaged by a crosscut saw, he said, "Mighty hot day for the law to be out and about. Didn't realize our fair city had come to the attention of the Texas Rangers. What can I do for you *gentlemen*?" He shot the word at us like he'd just spit a wad of phlegm the size of a hickory nut out on the top of the table.

Tipplers and gamblers closest to the door ducked their heads and skipped out. Left me with a lot less to worry about.

Boz grinned. "Figured we'd stop by and say hello, Longstreet. Get to know one another. Never hurts to be friendly. Even with skunks like you."

"I thought we had enough law in Iron Bluff. Town can't boast of but about three hundred people living in and around it. Ain't you boys got anything else to do, some other place to visit where you can harass peaceable sorts like me?" You didn't have to be too smart to hear the growing irritation and possible threat in the hired gunman's sand-and-gravel-filled response.

"No intent to harass you, Casper. Merely wanted to let you know we're in town and won't take kindly to gunfights, call-out shootings, or downright murder."

If what Boz said had any impact on the cadaverous killer, I couldn't tell it. He swatted at a bluebottle fly the size of a shot glass, twirled his drink around on the table, and said, "No need to be concerned, Rangers. I simply stopped by today to get out of the blistering sun and have a few drinks."

Heard all I needed when he started lying. I said, "That's not what we've been told. Rumor going around town says you're out to kill anyone handy from the Pitt camp today. Any truth to the story, or could it be you're simply a loose-mouthed blowhard who got jerked up short before you could act on an ill-considered idea?"

Well, by God, that one lit a fire under ole Casper. He sat bolt upright in his chair. Glared at me like he'd found a pimple on his pockmarked neck that needed to be popped and rendered out.

Ugly son of a bitch snapped, "I've killed more men than you can imagine, for a damned sight less than what you just said to me, boy. Ever rattle off like that at me again and I'll plant you in a heartbeat."

Boz snapped, "Damned nervy for a man with two shotguns loaded with buckshot trained on him, Casper. Besides, I'm not sure you could beat young Lucius in a straight-up gunfight anyway. Take some sincerely offered advice. Be righteously careful while we're visiting. We don't like dead citizens, regardless of how they get that way, but have no problem at all stamping out cockroaches of your sort."

Boz sounded serious as typhus up to that point. But then he got deadly. "Kill anyone and you'll have to deal with us, and I can guar-an-damn-tee you won't like the outcome, gunfighter."

We backed our way out onto the boardwalk, then started toward the jail. Boz stopped in the middle of the street and said, "Might as well have a word with Pitt's bunch at the Fin and Feather while we're at it. Same deal. Stay close and watch my back."

Marched into Romulus Pitt's personal watering hole, directly to the table where Nick Fox held court with at least half-a-dozen other men who bristled with pistols, knives, and all manner of other weaponry. Whole bunch looked madder than a nest of red wasps. Our appearance didn't do much toward leveling their mood out in the least.

Fox took little notice of us until we'd almost walked right up in his lap. Testy killer had removed his sweat-soaked hat and laid it on the table nearby. No hair on his head. Smooth as an ivory cue ball. Figured he probably shaved it every morning. Took everything I could do to keep from laughing. Knew if I did, lead would fly for sure.

Fox barely glanced at Boz and snorted, "What the hell

you want, Tatum? Hoped I might get through the day without having to see you."

Boz grinned and said, "Oops. Guess your day just ain't gonna turn out well at all, Nick."

"Get on with it then, you son of a bitch. What do you want? Know you didn't come into Mr. Pitt's saloon for a drink."

Moved to a spot that kept Boz out of my line of fire in case I had to blast someone at the table. Boz turned slightly to bring Fox under the gun and said, "Hear you boys might be getting ready for a fight with Casper Longstreet. Lucius and I just spoke with that sweet-natured soul. Warned him of how foolish it would be to indulge in such behavior when there are Rangers in town. Me, Lucius, and Rip don't take kindly to gunplay. Forced or otherwise. Be better if you reconsidered any thoughts you might have along those lines."

Man at the table I didn't know said, "You do what you have to do, Ranger Tatum. But know this, if that cadaverous son of a bitch pulls on me, I'll kill him deader than Davy Crockett, sure as I'm sittin' here talkin' to you."

I was standing directly behind the stranger when he popped off. Couldn't see his face. I said, "Who the hell are you, mister?"

He didn't even move. "Name's Alvin Clements. And while you bastards might have the bluff in on some of these other yahoos, don't try it on me. I'd just as soon blast you as anyone else."

Didn't matter that I couldn't see his face. Recognized the name. Another of Pitt's gunmen. Waited a second, and decided we had enough problems with Longstreet and Fox prowling around. So, I whacked Clements on the side of his head with the barrel of my shotgun and knocked his sorry ass about three feet. He bounced off the wall and dropped to his knees; ignoramus made a groggy-headed attempt to get up, so I whacked him again. Came to the conclusion that the Boz Tatum method worked. Clements had nothing more to add to the discussion at hand.

When he finally stopped moving, I looked at Boz and said, "We'll lock him in Marshal Stonehill's jail for a day or two. One less troublesome irritant to worry about."

Thought Boz might fall down laughing. Fox turned livid. Man's face colored up and he drew his right hand toward the edge of the table.

All Boz had to say was, "Wouldn't do that, Nick. Hate to pull this trigger and splatter you, and three or four others, all over hell and yonder. Real messy. Probably take Pitt's bartender and a swamper two, maybe three days to clean all the brains and guts off the wall."

While he made his speech, I searched Clements. Found four pistols, two knives, and a small hatchet. One of the pistols turned out to be a Le Mat black-powder thing popular with soldiers of the South during the Civil War. Big blaster fired nine .42-caliber shots from a regular barrel, and had a special chamber that carried a single round of buckshot. Nasty weapon for sure. But it takes all day to load one of them.

We made four of the cowboys at the table carry Clements over to Marshal Stonehill's jail. They grumbled and complained all the way, but didn't have much choice in the matter. We locked him in the best-looking cell I'd ever seen. Dismissed his friends, and settled in to wait for the marshal to return.

Cleanest, best-appointed marshal's office you could dream up. Leather-covered chairs, heavy mahogany desk, well-stocked gun rack, polished floors, and an overnight living space for the resident lawman that rivaled any ten-dollar-a-night hotel room.

Boz flopped into a chair, propped his feet on Stonehill's desk, and said, "Pitt's lawman lackey won't like this a bit. Bet he'll pop his cork when he gets back and sees who we've locked up."

Found me a comfortable corner and sat on the floor. Laid all my weapons out and rechecked the loads. Glanced up at Boz and said, "You know, we could save ourselves a lot of trouble and lock the marshal up too. I don't care overly much about having the local law sided up with folks who might try to end my life. Situation doesn't give me a real warm and comfortable feeling. Know what I mean?"

"Understand completely, Lucius. I'm afraid we can't just go and throw the town marshal in a cell for no particular reason. He could be a danger to us, true enough. But being dangerous ain't against the law. We've got to find some kind of believable legal reason to lock his sorry self up. Get him off the streets and out of our collective hair."

"You know, the more I think on it, Boz, locking Stonehill away might not be necessary. If he's as big a coward as Horace Breedlove described, maybe he'll just slink out of town when the going gets rough. No doubt in my mind, the worst we'll see here is still down the street and round the corner."

"Don't let Breedlove lead you in the wrong direction. Stonehill might be yellow. Then again, maybe he's just the cautious type. Didn't appear all that skittish when we met him. Could be he's the worst nightmare we could have while we're here. But I've never heard his name mentioned as a man to be wary of."

'Bout then Stonehill pushed the door open and stepped inside. Couldn't see us until his eyes adjusted to the dark room. Jerked back a bit and said, "What the hell are you two doing here?"

Boz said, "Had to find a place of incarceration for a

prisoner, Marshal. Being as how you have the only jail in town, we appropriated one of your cells to fulfill the needs of the state."

"Who'd you lock up?" Stonehill snapped.

Wanted to see if I could irritate him some more, so I said, "Alvin Clements."

Iron Bluff's resident enforcer of the law snatched his hat off and threw it on the floor. "What in the hell are you men thinking? Have you lost your pea-sized minds?" He kicked the hat across the room.

Boz waved a reassuring hand Stonehill's direction and said, "Calm down, Marshal. Nothing to get excited about."

Had absolutely no effect. "You can't be so stupid as to not know that Romulus Pitt pays my salary. Hell, almost everyone in Iron Bluff either works for, or is owned by, the man. He won't take this lying down. Bet you every penny I'm carrying in my pocket, before the sun sets, Pitt'll be standing right where I am now demanding I release Clements. What'll you do then?"

Boz pulled a penknife from his vest pocket and ceremoniously made quite a production of cleaning his fingernails. He kept at it for some seconds before finally saying, "Think I'd tell him to go next door to the Fin and Feather, have a drink, and relax a bit. 'Cause I ain't letting Clements go till I get good and ready. Figure ole Alvin needs a bit of seclusion so he can contemplate the future and his place in the universe according to Ranger Boz Tatum."

Stonehill threw up his hands in disgust. "You two nimrods don't have the least understanding of the situation here, do you?"

I glanced up from checking my shotgun and said, "We're getting there. Should have a fair handle on it in another week or so."

"No. You don't. Won't and can't," Stonehill countered.

"Pitt and his family hate the Tingwells. Feels they're little better than a pack of rabid, mange-ridden dogs. The Tingwells hate the Pitts. They believe Romulus and his boys are out to destroy them."

"Well, if that's what Bull and his bunch believe, they're probably right," Boz said.

Stonehill nodded. "There you go. These folks are building toward bloodlettin' the likes of which this part of Texas hasn't seen in twenty or thirty years. You men go meddling into the situation, by throwing either of their gunhands in jail for no good reason, and the whole shootin' match could break into open warfare."

Boz nodded his agreement, but said, "I've already come to the conclusion that we can't stop these two packs of angry wolves from tearing each other apart. Do believe, however, that we can slow the inevitable down some."

I jumped in with, "Pitt won't blow a gasket and start killing Tingwells because of what two Rangers did here today. He may rant and rave, but that'll be the end of it."

Stonehill's shoulders drooped. He took on the aspect of a beaten man. "I'm not a bad lawman, boys. Fact is, I'm a pretty damned good one. But I'll be the first to admit I'm no match for Hatch, Longstreet, Fox, or Clements in a stand-up gunfight. I have serious doubts either of you are. Romulus Pitt knows that. He may kill *me* for what you've done. And then kill both you as well."

"Relax, Bronson," Boz said. "My partner, Lucius "By God" Dodge, is faster than anyone I've ever seen—except me, of course. And we're both meaner'n rabid coyotes. Ain't that so, Lucius?"

Stonehill stomped across the office, gathered his hat off the floor, and headed for the door. He latched onto the brass knob, turned back to us, and said, "My sister owns a nice spread between here and Lone Pine. Think I'll head over that way for a few days. Sit on her porch and drink cold water from her deep well. Wait till you boys are dead. Then I'll come back."

"You can do that? Just take off without so much as a by-your-leave to your boss?" I asked.

"Mighty nice arrangement you've got here, I'd say. What'll we tell Pitt if he asks of your whereabouts?" Boz seemed mighty pleased with himself. We were about to get rid of another problem without having fired a shot.

"Tell him you don't know. Tell him I'd already been gone a day or so when you set up shop in his jail. Whatever you decide to tell him, I don't want to be around when he kills you boys. Think I can take care of myself, in most situations, but I'd just as soon not have the Texas Rangers snappin' at my heels for the rest of my natural life." The door slammed—and Stonehill vanished.

Boz said, "Well, ain't that a corker. Seems we just inherited us a jail. Damned fine one at that. Bet Romulus Pitt's gonna be madder'n a rained-on rooster when he finds out what just transpired. Course I ain't gonna be the one to tell him. How 'bout you, Lucius? You gonna tattle on Iron Bluff's brave marshal?"

"A man's gotta do whatever he feels is right, Boz. Too bad he didn't have enough spine to act like a real lawman. Should have hooked up with us and done what really is the right thing. Personally, I don't know how Stonehill can look at himself in the shavin' mirror every morning."

We sat around for about an hour patting ourselves on the back about how great everything had turned out. Cooked some coffee and were looking forward to a setting sun and the coolness of evening.

Ragged nasty-looking cloud bank settled over the river and covered the town as well. Got between us and a scorching sun. Temperature must have dropped a whopping two or three degrees. A welcome break for sure. Figured by eight or nine in the evening things might get almost comfortable. Hoped for rain, didn't hold my breath.

Barely got settled good when half-a-dozen pistol shots shattered our misplaced feelings of contentment. Barrage was so close to the jailhouse it almost broke the windows out. Rattled 'em all like a cannon shot on the Fourth of July. Set us to grabbing for our shotguns and scampering for the door.

7

"Let's Hang the Murderin' Bastard"

BOZ GRABBED THE brass knob and said, "You take a gander, Lucius. See if you can tell what's happening. Once we've got the lay of it, I'll go out first. We'll head for the wall on the right. Stay behind me and cover my back."

He cracked the door open, and all I could see was a heavy cloud of drifting gun smoke mixed with copper-colored dust carried on a light breeze. Peeked around the corner toward the Fin and Feather. John Roman Hatch, the only hired killer in town who hadn't been on the receiving end of our sharply delivered cautions that afternoon, stood in the street holding a smoking pistol in each hand.

"Think it's Hatch, Boz. Man I can see is wearing a red silk vest and black felt gambler's hat trimmed with hammered silver conchos. Tall black boots just like Rip said."

"Does he seem to have finished his business, Lucius?"

"Doesn't appear that way to me, Boz. Son of a bitch is cocked, primed, and coiled up like a diamondback rattler.

Probably end up like the poor goober on the other end of his pistols if we go out now."

"See any victims?"

"Somebody's laying facedown on the walk in front of the saloon. I can't tell who it is, though. Hatch ain't backing off. Man's rooted to a single spot. Looks like he's ready for another killing."

Boz snorted. "Shit, wait till he looks down the wrong end of this ten-gauge monster. Murderin' skunk will get religion right damned quick."

Before I could stop him, my partner pushed me out of the doorway and darted onto the jail's covered porch. The unexpected movement startled Hatch. Don't think he ever really saw Boz—just a blur at the edges of his vision.

Pistolero's right hand swung our way and spit flame and smoke three times, so fast I could barely count them. One shot took a chunk, the size of my hand, out of the door frame. Second snapped Boz's hat off, and the last singed a path up the skin on my friend's left arm, from the knuckles on his hand to his elbow. Don't know to this day what kept him from getting killed.

The thing that amazed me, more than Boz's amazing luck, was how he stood his ground. Man didn't even flinch as blood began to dribble from his dangling arm and pool up at his feet. Any other Ranger in his situation would have sent John Roman Hatch to hell, in several different pieces on an outhouse door. Not Boz.

Roar from his big blaster delivered a wad of hot lead pellets about a yard in front of Hatch's booted feet. Carefully delivered shot kicked a cloud of red dust the size of a horse into the astonished killer's face.

Still holding the coach gun in his good hand, Boz yelled, "Holster your weapons, Hatch. Put 'em away or I'll turn you into something even your mother won't recognize."

I slipped up behind my wounded friend and added two more barrels of heavy-gauge potential death to his argument against further gunfire. Hatch spit an egg-sized ball of phlegm into the hole at his feet, and turned ever so slightly to get a better view of who'd fired at him.

We had to squint, because the afternoon sun sat right on the roof line of the Matador across the street. Made it a bit more difficult to see the Tingwells' hired assassin from where we stood, but not enough to keep him alive if he made the wrong move.

"Sorry about my misplaced response, boys, but you Rangers got no place in this argument. Stay the hell out of it. These two jackasses made a serious error in judgment and paid a lethal price. Long as the rest of Pitt's bunch stay inside and behave, there'll be no more gunplay."

Boz jumped off the porch and took about six steps toward Hatch. Stunned the hell out of me. Happened so fast I could barely keep up with him. "I ain't gonna say this again. Holster your weapons, you son of a bitch, or we'll kill you where you stand." Couldn't have been any doubt, for even the most casual observer, that Boz Tatum was right on the knife's edge of sending John Roman Hatch for the Lord God Almighty's final eternal judgment.

While faster than greased lightning with a brace of Colts, Hatch was also one of the smarter gunfighters I've run across over the years. He looked down three barrels of buckshot and immediately had a soul-saving conversion of Biblical proportions.

"Hold on now. Hardware's going in their holsters. Ain't gonna be no more shooting, long as the rest of Pitt's gang of idiots keep their heads." Unruffled professional killer did a fancy spin with his long-barreled cavalry-model Colts and delivered both to waiting holsters nested high on his hips.

Boz let out a sharp breath of relief and said, "Walk up as close as you can get, Lucius. Keep your gun on him while I try and stem a bit of this bleeding."

I got to within spitting distance of Hatch before he spoke. "Hell, I didn't want to kill these boys. Tied my horse in front of the Matador and had started inside for a drink, when these two waddies went to yelling at me from about where you see 'em now. They called me a low-life, cow-flop-eatin' son of a bitch. Made filthy allusions as to the chastity of my dear sainted mother, and questioned the legitimacy of my birth. Ain't no man living gonna call my mother a whore—and live out the day. Damn sight more'n any Southern gentleman of goodwill should have to put up with."

Boz strolled up and barked, "I'll take them pistols, Hatch." Gunfighter obviously hated such instructions, but how are you gonna argue with a man holding the open end of a shotgun against your guts? John Roman handed his weapons over right gingerly.

Boz said, "I'll lock him up, Lucius. See if you can find any witnesses to this mess."

"What the hell are you talking about? There ain't no call to put me in jail. These jackasses started it. Picked the fight, and then pulled on me first."

Boz almost laughed in the man's face. Said, "Damned if I'll take your word on two killings, Hatch. Soon as we've done with our investigation, and maybe an inquest, I don't have any doubt you'll be released to kill some more. But right now, you're gonna sit in a cell for a few days."

Hatch went livid. "The hell you say."

"Yes, by God. The hell I *do* say."

Then our prisoner picked the wrong time to get belliger-ent. "I'll just be goddamned if that's so. You try it and there'll be hell to pay, Tatum."

That's when Boz whacked him across the noggin with

the barrel of his shotgun. Hatch joined his shadow in the dirt. As Boz breeched the huge weapon and reloaded the spent barrel he said, "Grab one of his feet, Lucius. We'll drag him. Soon as we've got him secured, I'm gonna go looking for a sawbones to fix this crease he put in me. Want you to check around for witnesses."

We dumped Hatch's limp carcass in the cell next to Alvin Clements. Needless to say, Clements protested. "I don't want that sorry piece of festerin' scuz next to me. Ain't no one in East Texas I hate more'n John Roman Hatch. Hell, boys, you're creatin' yourself a real problem by doin' somethin' this stupid."

So, we moved Hatch to the third cell, which put an empty one between them. Clements wasn't a whole bunch happier. He leaned on his barred door and said, "That ain't no better, Boz. I don't want him in here with me."

Boz reached between the bars with his bloody hand, grabbed Clements by the throat, lifted him up on his toes, and snapped, "Shut your mouth, or I'll come in there and shut it for you. I've had a headache ever since we rode into this jerkwater burg. Now I've been shot. Please believe me when I say, you wouldn't like it should I have to kick your bony ass. Besides, there ain't no other place for him right now and you damn well know it." When Boz turned him loose, Clements fell into his cot, but I could tell he didn't like being humiliated again one damned bit.

By the time we got back out to the Fin and Feather's piece of boardwalk, a sizable crowd had gathered around the dead men. One of the spectators turned out to be the town's resident pill-roller. Right nice gent named Leonard Adamson. He'd already checked on John Roman Hatch's handiwork. Pronounced both them fellers deader than rotten stumps. Took Boz to his office over next to the bank and went right to work on him.

I talked with a number of townsfolk who claimed to have witnessed the shootings. Old-timer named Felthus Runyon declared as how he'd come out of the Matador just as the skirmish pimpled to a nasty head. "Yessir. Seen the hull show. Heerd ever word what got said. You see, young feller, them cowboys comed out'n the Fin and Feather some drunked up and a lot stupid. Went to raggin' on 'at 'ere gunfighter Hatch. Not too smort, if'n you ask me. Called him some pert filthy names. Went to mouthin' off 'bout the man's mother and sech. Appeared to me as though Mr. Hatch tried to avoid the thang. Couldn't do 'er. Them boys seemed determined to die 'fer as I could see."

His story sounded almost to the letter of Hatch's own rendition of the killings. But friends, over the years I've come to have little trust in eyewitness accounts of such events. As is the case with most of them, you can always find someone who just didn't see it the same way.

Young man wearing a derby hat and suit said, "My name's Andrew Nash. I'm a teller over in the Texas State Bank. Was on my way home for dinner when this incident unfolded. John Roman Hatch caused the whole thing. Soon as he tied his animal, these poor guiltless souls came out of the Fin and Feather and went to saddle up. Hatch called them out and shot both men like dogs." Being as how Romulus Pitt's name appeared on the bank's window as being the owner, I tended not to believe Nash's version of the shooting.

Same with all the other witnesses. If a body didn't know any better, you'd have thought the entire sober population of Iron Bluff had been on the street when the bloody episode occurred and had seen every second as it unfolded. Split right down the middle on what happened. Half agreed with Runyon. Other half sided with Nash.

Then, as if on cue, Pitt's remaining bunch of riders

poured out of the Fin and Feather, flooded the street, and went to hollering stuff like, "It was cold-blooded murder." And, "What we need here, by God, is a dose of oak tree justice." And, "Hell, we don't have to wait. Git a rope. Let's hang the murderin' bastard."

Nick Fox led the chorus, and it appeared the situation was about to get beyond my meager control, when Boz showed up again. His left arm was professionally dressed, but if it bothered the man you couldn't tell it. He walked up beside me and said, "Let's put all four shots over their heads. Get their attention. Reload quick as you can."

Raised our shotguns and fired into the air. Dumped our empties and were ready for more action in a flash. God Almighty, people went to running and screaming like Gabriel had just blown his horn and announced the Second Coming. Town folk abandoned Pitt's riders to an empty street, the company of two angry Rangers, and a pair of dead men. Happened so fast, those Pitt riders didn't know which way to turn.

Boz gave them all the guidance they needed when he yelled, "You men saddle up and get back to the Pitt ranch. No need of you here. We'll take care of this and see to it the law is served."

Fox looked totally unfazed by the turn of events. He slipped his hands into the waist of his pants in an obvious move to indicate he wanted no part of a quarrel with our shotguns. But I could tell he wasn't about to let the evening's events go without letting us know how he felt.

Black-draped gunman swelled up and said, "Damned if we'll leave till there's some satisfaction fer what John Roman Hatch did. McCall and Wheeler weren't a match for a killer of his skill on the best day the two of 'em ever had."

I couldn't resist the temptation to goad the man a bit just to see what would happen. Said, "And I suppose you must think you are a match for Hatch. Is that it, Nick? Want us to turn him loose and see which of you is left after another face-off like this one?"

His face reddened up. "I never said that. But if the situation ever arises, can gar-un-damn-tee you I'm more'n a match for John Roman than anyone else in town these days." He tilted his head toward the still-oozing corpses on the Fin and Feather's boardwalk. "These boys wasn't nothin' but drovers. Ain't no way in hell they picked a fight with that murderin' skunk."

Boz pulled the same trick again. Walked right up in his adversary's face, placed the muzzle of the ten-gauge against the buckle of Fox's pistol belt, and said, "That ain't the way witnesses tell it, Nick. So you take your men and get back out to the Pitt ranch right now. I don't want to see any of you on the street before day after tomorrow. If I do you'll answer to me, and I'm faster, meaner, and a damn sight more deadly than any of you mouthy sons of bitches."

Fox almost choked right on the spot. Coughed and snapped, "Bet Ole Man Pitt will have plenty to say about this."

I stepped up beside Boz and said, "You tell him, if he wants to talk with us, to come in alone. You and the rest of this crew show up with him and most of you won't do another thing in this world. Got the message, gunhand?"

His upper lip peeled back. "I heard you, Dodge. Come on, boys. Let's head for the ranch. We'll let Mr. Pitt take care of these skunks."

Whole damned bunch saddled up and stormed out of town in a fog of dust and horse sweat. Me and Boz made the final arrangements for the dead men. We talked with at least a dozen more folks who claimed to have seen the whole shooting match. Much to our surprise, and dismay, almost all of them confirmed John Roman's version of the story. We placed our greatest faith in Cloud Quigley. He owned, managed, and edited the *Iron Bluff Weekly Sentinel*. Not much of a newspaper, but the only one in town.

Boz caught him in front of the *Sentinel*'s tiny office just at dusk. Quigley's open front door had had a clear view of the entire incident. He said, "Well, I'd just walked past the door. Heard men yelling."

"Was the door open or closed at the time?" Boz asked.

"Open. Hell, it's so hot can't stand to close it for very long. All the windows, back door, everything I can expose to any moving air is open. Plays hell on my typesetting, but can't be helped."

"What did you see, Mr. Quigley?" I asked.

"Men on the boardwalk in front of Romulus Pitt's saloon were yelling the foulest kind of obscenities at someone on this side of the street. I had to come out here where we're standing now to see who they were baiting."

Boz glanced down toward the Matador and pointed. "Hatch says he tied his horse over there. You sure them boys were out to pick a fight? Seems a stupid thing to do, don't it?"

"They looked drunk to me. Hell, you know how it is, Ranger Tatum. Put enough of the right kind of skull-popper in the meekest mouse you can find and sometimes, at just the exact wrong moment, that tiny rodent will go toe-to-toe with the biggest, meanest, yellow-stripped tomcat in Texas."

Scratched my head and said, "You think that's what happened here? The mice took on the wrong cat?"

"Sure seemed so. Like most, I've heard tales of what a cold-blooded killer Hatch is. But in this instance, he did just about everything he could to avoid a fight. Doubt you could find a man in town who would've suffered those fools to run off at the mouth the way they did before something happened."

"You willing to testify to what you've just said?" Boz asked.

"Most assuredly, sir. But I can't imagine why anyone who saw this would need to testify. Open-and-shut case of self-defense. After all the verbal abuse, Wheeler and McCall drew first. Hatch even let them have the opening round of shots. Don't know if you heard it, but if you did, think about it. There were two rounds of gunfire. First one came from the dead men. They missed. Then Hatch blasted the hell out of them. Swear 'fore God, that's the way it happened. At least that's the way I saw it."

We thanked Quigley for his testimony, and then headed back to the jail. Sat around and patted ourselves on the back for the way things had turned out that afternoon. Bloody event could have been a lot worse. Especially if Nick Fox and Pitt's other riders had managed to have their way.

Got quiet, for a second or so, before Boz said, "Figure Ole Man Pitt will be riding in soon. Bet he'll want us to turn Clements loose and hang Hatch as soon as possible. Got his riders stretched out on boards behind the barbershop. Kind of thing can really get a man like Pitt all humped up and kicking."

Romulus Pitt failed to fulfill my partner's prediction. But Bull Tingwell hit the door about seven o'clock that evening like a Kansas cyclone bent on destroying everything in its path. Old man was smart enough to leave his idiot sons and hired followers back at the ranch, but failed when it came to reining in his mouth.

He stomped up to the desk, all red in the face and shaking. Shook a knotty finger in Boz's face and damn near screamed, "You've got John Roman Hatch locked up in this hellhole and I want him out right goddamned now."

Boz grinned and said, "Well, why don't you wish in one hand and shit in the other and see which one fills up the quickest."

God Almighty, I thought that old man's head was gonna pop open like a festered boil. He snatched his hat off and shook it at Boz. "Look you here, maggot. Casper Longstreet seen what went on out in front of the Fin and Feather this afternoon. According to him it were a straight-up fair fight and wuz brung on by two stupid waddies of Pitt's. Ain't no reason for you to keep my man Hatch in a jail cell. Never should have locked him up to begin with."

Had me one of Marshal Stonehill's expensive leather thrones pulled over in my favorite corner. Kind of straightened up, and when I did the chair creaked. Don't think Tingwell had seen me up till then.

I said, "Be that as it may, Mr. Tingwell, he is behind bars and he'll stay that way till my partner decides otherwise. Could be a spell, old man. You might as well get used to it."

Ole Bull swelled up like a swamp-dwelling frog on the verge of exploding. "You don't understand," he croaked, "There's a war a-coming. I need him. Pitt's bringing in new people to take his side every day. Right now, all I've got in the way of professional help is Hatch and Longstreet. They could be the difference in whether me and my family stay alive. You've got no call to keep Hatch in jail fer defending himself."

Almost passed out when Boz said, "Tell you what, old man, I'll trade your gunfighter for Miss Ruby Black. Bring me the girl, unharmed, and you can have John Roman the moment her foot crosses the threshold of the door you just came through."

My God, but it got awful quiet for almost a minute. Only thing making any noise were the crickets outside.

Bull Tingwell looked like he'd been hit in the face with a dead cat. Hell, I probably looked just as surprised. Wouldn't have thought of such a thing myself in a hundred years. But I had to admit, it was a stroke of near genius.

Tingwell came out of deep thought, scratched his rough chin, and said, "Done told you afore, I don't know nothing of the whereabouts of that young woman. She left town on the westbound stage, so far as I be a-knowin'."

Boz leaned back in his chair, put his feet up on Stone-hill's desk like a man about to take a nap. "Got no reason not to believe you, Bull. But the offer still goes. There's only one qualifier. She's got to be here by morning, or I'll just forget the whole thing and start looking for a judge or justice of the peace to come in and conduct an inquest into the shooting. Could be he might bind Hatch over for trial. Your gunman's future might very well include a long rope—and a short fall."

For the first time Tingwell smiled. "We have a judge right here in Iron Bluff, pretty good one too. Don't seem to favor either Romulus Pitt or me in any of our disputes in the past. I wouldn't be a-havin' no problem with him hearing the case."

Could see where Boz intended for his bluff to go, so I said, "Better if we bring in our own judge, I think. Boz and I have access to an honest and well-respected member of the Texas bar in Judge Stanley Cooper of Shelbyville. He'd be more than willing to preside over any of the legalities we determine might be necessary to clear this mess up."

"But like I mentioned before," Boz said, "whole matter could be taken care of with the appearance of Miss Black in this office no later than tomorrow morning."

Tingwell grunted, "Uh-huh." He spun around on his heel and stomped out the door. We could hear his horse gallop away.

I turned to Boz and said, "Jesus, where'd all this business of a trade come from?"

He grinned. "Don't know. Maybe it was some kind of divine intervention. Thought just popped into my head. Given what we learned from the witnesses, I could've easily let Hatch go on his merry way earlier today. Only reason I threw him in a cell was to get him off the street. But when Bull showed up, it occurred to me John Roman might just serve a greater purpose."

"Yeah, but if we turn him loose, might well occur that we'll have to kill him later."

"I know, Lucius. But it'd be worth getting the girl back without a fight, don't you think? Even with a court order in hand, way I had it figured, we'd still have to shoot a bloody path into the Tingwell place to get her out. It'd be a damned dangerous prospect for any party being held captive by that bunch of brainless yahoos."

I couldn't argue with such reasoning. Said, "Well, guess we'll find out just how bad ole Bull wants his hired gunny back. Sun will be up no later than six tomorrow morning. Think I'll get me a little sleep. Next few hours have the potential for some mighty interesting events."

Threw my bedroll on the floor in front of the desk. Piled my pistol belt in the chair. Boz dropped off into dreamland stretched out in his new leather seat before I could get myself situated. Actually, I tried not to sleep, but couldn't help myself. Know it was several hours later, but felt like I had barely closed my eyes for no more than a few seconds, when the door of the jail creaked open. Sound snapped me out of my nap like a bucket of cold water in the face.

Most beautiful woman I'd ever seen stepped into the room like a lost child. Think I fell in love with her soon as I laid eyes on Ruby Black. She appeared scratched, beat-up, dazed, confused, unwashed, and on the verge of running and screaming. At first I thought I was still asleep and dreaming of red-haired angels, or maybe a lost ghost sent to haunt dark corners of my heart.

She held out a trembling hand, gazed down at me with vacant eyes, and said, "Would you be good enough to help me, sir?"

8

"If Either One of Us Scared Him, I Couldn't Tell It"

I SCRAMBLED AROUND on the floor like a startled turtle. Got tangled up in my bedding, and almost knocked my chair over before stumbling to my sock feet. As I reached for the specter's pale hand, a jolt of blue flame shot from her quavering finger to mine. Spark sizzled and popped through the dense air. When I snatched my hand away, a feeble smile played across her lips.

"Bless me, that's never happened before," she mumbled.

Moved guns and other gear around, and led her to the empty seat. All the noise and movement woke Boz. He turned the wick up on our lantern. Ruby Black's otherworldly materialization seemed to have as profound an effect on my friend as it did on me. He recovered quicker.

"You are Miss Ruby Black, aren't you?" he asked.

"Yes. I'm Ruby Black." She could barely speak, and stared into emptiness as though a large part of her was not there with us.

Then, Boz almost whispered the question I'm certain would have proved difficult for me to ask. "Have you been harmed in any way, Miss Black?" An abundance of hidden concern lay in Boz's gentle query.

"No." Then she paused for some seconds and appeared to search for the right words. Cracked lips tried to form an added response, but nothing came out. She glanced up at me, as if asking for my help again. I felt drawn into a pair of the most astonishing turquoise eyes I'd ever seen.

From somewhere far away, I heard my own voice. "Should we rouse Doc Adamson, Miss Black?"

When no response came, I asked the question another way. "Do you need the attentions of a doctor, miss?"

Long-lashed eyelids flickered in mystification several times before she responded. "No. I've not been harmed. At least not in the way you might imagine."

Boz said, "Wag Culpepper sent us to find you, miss. He and your family are very concerned about your well-being. I'll get a telegram off to Ranger Headquarters in Fort Worth as soon as I can this morning. Feel certain your family will be advised of these events by no later than noon today."

She slumped in one of the chairs and covered her eyes with a trembling hand. "I do thank you, sir. Would it be possible for me to lie down for a short time? Feels as if I haven't slept since the day I arrived here."

I grasped the shattered girl by the elbow and gently guided her from her seat. The warmth beneath my hand crept up my arm—and spread. "Please take the bed in the corner, miss. I'll rig up a curtain to give you some solitude. While you nap, we'll clear out two of the cells in back and arrange a place of even more privacy."

The exhausted girl fell into Marshal Stonehill's narrow cot as though she'd been shot. Do believe sleep hit before her head touched the pillow.

We stretched a length of rope across the room and draped blankets over it. Ruby Black didn't so much as twitch the whole time we worked. On several occasions she talked in her sleep, but I could never make out exactly what she whispered through barely parted lips. Once it got so quiet I sent Boz to check on her for fear she might have died or something.

A bit later, when I asked him to look in on her, he said, "You're the one what's worried. You go check." From then on, it was as though he'd decided to leave Ruby Black's complete care to me. Think that's what really sealed my fate. Every time I looked at her stunning face, something magical burned through my veins, turned my blood to liquid fire, and made my head spin.

Boz fetched John Roman Hatch out of his cell. Brought him up front and handed the gunman his pistol belt. Killer still sported a nasty-crusted knot on his head. Cut in the middle had scabbed over with black-tinged blood. Wound made wearing a hat some painful for him. Tried to hide my smile, but didn't have much luck at it.

Boz said, "You're one lucky joker, John Roman. Gonna give you a pass on what happened out front yesterday. May hold an inquest sometime in the future, but right now, we've got other fish to fry."

In about as short a tone as a body could muster, I added, "Get out of town for a few days. Don't go gunning for anyone else. Next time, we won't be forgiving enough to let you have three shots at a Texas Ranger before sending you to God."

My speech had no discernible effect on Hatch. He snorted like a mad bull and snapped, "I'll let you in on a little secret, Rangers. While I do appreciate my freedom, I ain't about to let any of Romulus Pitt's gang of cowboys and killers publicly heap insults on my head and then shoot me down like a rabid dog."

Boz got red in the face and was about to respond when I jumped in again. "My friend has given you some reasonable, and extremely charitable, instructions for future behavior, Hatch. I'll put it another way. Next time you shoot anyone in Iron Bluff, I'll personally kill you deader than a can of store-bought corned beef."

Hatch glanced up at me from buckling his pistol belt. "Better keep your attack dog on a leash, Tatum. I've been known to stomp pups like this one to death for a damned sight less than I've already heard."

He didn't slow me even a smidgen. "There won't be any friendly arrest and overnight jail stay next time, gunfighter. I'll personally see to it you're planted facedown, and deep, after I put enough holes in your sorry ass to read the *San Augustine Times* through."

Boz grabbed Hatch by the shirtfront and jerked the smart-talking assassin up, nose to nose. "Weren't for giving my word to your employer, I'd shoot you right here right now myself. Never could stand your kind of mean-mouthed jackass. Do exactly what we just told you. See your ugly face in less than three days, and you'll discover me and my attack dog don't make idle threats."

If either one of us scared him, I couldn't tell it. He smirked his way to the door and disappeared ahead of the insolent sound of jingling spurs. Heavy cloud of tension followed the murderous thug.

Boz shook his head. He leaned against the desk and said, "Might as well roust Clements out too. Never did have a real good reason to hold him anyway. Been thinking our situation over, Lucius. I've come to the conclusion, if we affect the balance between Tingwell and Pitt much, one or the other of them will find such a temptation too hard to pass up, and will surely take advantage of it. We could have a slew of killings in a heartbeat."

"Fine by me if you want to let him go," I said. "Root that scum out. Miss Black can have the whole back part of the jail to herself that much quicker. Best place for her, I think. Would be willing to bet Morgan Tingwell didn't let her go willingly."

Boz's head snapped up like he'd been slapped. "You're probably right. I hadn't thought of it quite that way, though. It would be easier to keep an eye on the girl, so long as she's close by. And the jail is much safer than a hotel room or boardinghouse."

"Ladies in town might gossip over their back fences some, Boz. You know how women can be—two men and a beautiful young girl, in a confined area and all. But I'd feel better if she stayed here with us. Morgan Tingwell looked just crazy enough to come try and take her back."

Boz smiled. "Better for you too. Ain't that right, Lucius?" Then he got thoughtful for a second before saying, "Well, it's decided. We'll keep her in the cell block. Make sure she's armed when we're out and about. Way this heap of stones is put together, it'd take an army with a six-pound cannon to get inside."

Clements acted right cheery when we opened his cell door and told him he could hoof it. Boz gave Romulus Pitt's anxious hireling pretty much the same message about future behavior. His response was as different as night and day from John Roman Hatch's. Nodded his agreement, tipped his hat, and hit the door running.

"That went well," I said.

"Don't let his contrite behavior fool you, pard. In addition to being a man-killer, Clements is a low-life sneak who'll say, or do, anything to make you think he wouldn't harm a fly."

"Sure didn't seem like that when I whacked him on the head in the Matador."

"That was before he understood we meant what we said. From now on Alvin Clements will require serious watching on our part. Think we should exercise warier behavior in the future. Right now, I feel Clements is more dangerous than ever."

"How's that?"

"Before you bounced your shotgun barrel off his head, he would have gone at either of us—toe-to-toe. Now we're gonna have to watch our backs."

Being as how the jail had emptied out, me and Boz set to work and fixed Miss Black a nicely appointed private area in the last cell. He got all fussy and allowed as how he wanted to make the girl as comfortable as possible.

We went at it like a pair of field hands on a mission. Hung blankets from the bars, brought in a small table and chair, washbasin, soap, towels, and such. Boz even stepped out for a few minutes and cut some flowers out of somebody's garden when they weren't looking. Never knew him to display such sensibilities before, but the arrangement that rough-as-a-cob Ranger put together in Marshal Stonehill's glass water pitcher looked right nice.

We had to wake Ruby and help her make the move. Lethargic steps made her look like one of those opium fiends after a binge on the laudanum bottle. Girl acted like she couldn't get her eyes opened. Collapsed right inside the cell door, before either of us could offer our assistance. I lifted her into a bed that we'd softened up with an extra mattress.

Boz arranged the skirts over her scuffed lace-up black boots, stepped back, and said, "Blasted, sorry damned shame. Can't wait to hear the story she's got to tell, but I'm damned if I'll press her on the thing."

"Why's that, Boz?"

" 'Cause if Morgan Tingwell had his way with this poor

child, I'll have to kill the son of a bitch for damned sure.
Wag would expect it. He'd never say it, but he'd expect it.
Bet ole Bull wouldn't like me puttin' holes in his stupid son
one bit, though."

Both of us thought we'd had enough excitement for one
day. Course our feelings didn't mean a damned thing to
Romulus Pitt. He came storming into town again, at the
head of a mob of cowboys that appeared to have grown
some since his first visit. We heard them rumbling toward
us long before they arrived. Gave us plenty of time to get
prepared for whatever the arrogant bastard had in mind.

When the Pitt gang thundered to a stop in front of the
jail, we'd taken up spots on either side of the door, shotguns at the ready. Nick Fox rode between Eli and Pruitt
Pitt. Alvin Clements was nowhere to be seen. Man proved
smarter than I'd come to expect—at least in that instance.

The elder Pitt didn't waste any time with a shake and
howdy. Sat his tall dun horse like a swelled toad. Got right
to the point.

"Well, Tatum, hear you opened the door on Tingwell's
hired killer early this morning."

"No point holdin' him, Mr. Pitt. Way most folks told it,
leastways them we figured were impartial in their observa-
tions, Hatch didn't start the dance, merely finished it. Your
men caused the whole thing. Those poor boys got dead of
their own accord."

Before Romulus could respond, son Eli stood in his stirrups, shook a braided quirt at Boz, and said, "That's a
wagon load of horse dung and you know it, Tatum. That
villain murdered our men in cold blood. Our poor dead
boys didn't have no more chance than a pair of snowballs
in Reynosa during an August heat wave. Way I heard it, he
gunned 'em down like dogs, before they could even clear
leather."

I said, "Well, you heard it wrong, Eli."

Guess he didn't care for my assessment. Turned my direction and sniffed, "Wasn't talking to you, Dodge. If I want your opinion, I'll get down and beat it out of you."

Boz busted out laughing. His raucous reaction unnerved the tart-mouthed boy, and some of the others behind Romulus. The old man held a steadying hand out and waved his mouthy son into silence.

Boz said, "Listen to me, Eli. Climb off your animal for a dustup with Lucius, and I can guarantee your family will most certainly be attending a funeral tomorrow."

Whole scene got real tense and mighty quiet for a spell. Old Man Pitt fumed like a boiling pot jerked away from the fire. Finally he said, "I've had a bellyful of Bull Tingwell, his family of chuckleheads, and his hired killers. Hatch murdered two of my men, less than fifty feet from where we are this very minute. Killed them right in front of my own saloon, for the love of God. If you won't do anything about this assassination, then I can assure you we will."

Boz let a moment of silence follow the angry man's overconfident pronouncement before he spoke. What he said came out slow, deliberate, and threatening. "Best careful up, Mr. Pitt. Murder is murder. Hatch was defending himself and we've got witnesses, some of your leading citizens in fact, who will gladly testify to that fact. You or your boys track him down and do anything stupid, rest assured we'll be coming for payment."

Pruitt Pitt, who'd been silent up to that point, growled, "Gonna take more'n two half-assed Texas Rangers to keep us from doing as we damn well please, Tatum. Hatch has been moved to the top of our list of our most hated enemies. We will find Hatch, and Pitt family justice will be served, whether you like it or not. Come on, Pa. No point talking any further with these jackasses."

Romulus Pitt slumped in his saddle as if hit by a wave of exhaustion. He glanced at Boz, then me, from under the wide brim of his palm-leaf sombrero and said, "Hoped you boys would see the circumstances differently. Since you can't, we'll go our own way regarding the matter."

Entire group wheeled their sweaty animals around and roared out of town in a cloud of swirling dust, barking dogs, and squealing kids who chased them down the street throwing rocks.

Boz turned to me and said, "Damnation, I'm glad that's over."

"You think they'll do what they've threatened?" I asked.

"Could be, but Hatch ain't the man to work such ill-reasoned silliness on."

"Way I feel too. How do you think they'll try to get at him?"

"Well, if Pitt, or his sons, confronts John Roman head-on, it'll be the biggest mistake they ever make. Be more likely Romulus will send someone, like Fox or Clements, out for an ambush. It's a hell of a lot harder to prove anything when there ain't no witnesses. That's why we've got to keep our eyes open. Wouldn't surprise me one bit if either family had similar plans for the two of us."

I fell into one of the cane-backed chairs near our front door. Said, "I'll take the first watch, Boz. While I'm sure you're right, it's gonna be a spell before I can get comfortable with it."

The rest of a gloomy Texas afternoon moseyed in hot, dry, and miserable. We took turns guarding the street from our chunk of boardwalk.

About six o'clock Ruby woke up. She freshened herself with a spot of water and soap. And from somewhere unseen, must have produced a bit of perfume. Delicate scent of lilac preceded the girl when she joined us in the office.

I kept her company while Boz fetched a meal from Hermione Blackstock's café on the opposite side of the street from the jail.

Hermione called her ham-and-egg joint the White House Café. A pure exaggeration. Her place looked more like a made-over stable than our nation's capital. But, my God, that woman could cook. Hadn't been for Hermione, me and Boz would probably have starved to death during our stay in Iron Bluff.

Proper use of a knife and fork aided Ruby as she wolfed down most of a half-dozen eggs, a mound of bacon, four biscuits, a big gob of butter, a jar of muscadine jelly, and a pot of black coffee. I couldn't keep my eyes off her. She ate like a starving, but well-mannered, wildcat. Hell, I liked the way that beautiful gal made no effort to hide a healthy appetite. Her muscadine-tinted lips caused me to sweat like a man in a South Texas pepper-eating contest.

By the time she downed most of Hermione's rustic breakfast, that gal's cheeks got rosy again and she started acting like she felt a lot better. We waited until she'd almost finished before asking any questions. Ruby Black had one hell of a yarn to tell. Just hearing it was enough to make my flesh pimple up and crawl.

9

"Somebody Done Went and Lynched 'Em"

PERSONALLY, DIDN'T THINK he had to do it, but Boz tried to soft-glove the starved girl into her story. She was still gnawing on a strip of bacon and piece of biscuit when he said, "Miss Black, we've got to ask you some questions about your whereabouts this past month or so."

"I understand. And you may call me Ruby, Ranger." She swallowed daintily before issuing those instructions. Then the famished girl wiped sensuous lips on the back of her hand, threw a coy glance up at me, smiled, and went back to her meal.

Naturally, I wanted as much of her attention as could be had, so I said, "I'm Lucius Dodge, miss. My friend's name is Boz Tatum. Where'd you meet Morgan Tingwell, Miss Black?"

She flicked crumbs from the corner of her mouth and said, "Pleased to make your acquaintance, gentlemen. Morgan boarded my stage in Louisiana. In Alexandria, I believe. My traveling companion was taken ill in Baton Rouge and could not continue the trip. I decided to make do, and continue alone."

Boz scratched his beard. "A bit bold for a young lady in a strange place, wasn't it?"

A marked look of amazement flashed across her face. She placed both hands in her lap, smoothed the wrinkles out of her dress, and spoke to Boz as though he might still wear short pants. "I am a Texas woman, and have made the journey to and from New Orleans several times before, Ranger Tatum. There has been no problem in the past. I could foresee no reason to suspect anything like the events that occurred."

She appeared on the verge of a lecture. I said, "We mean no disrespect, Miss Black. You must admit, however, it is somewhat unusual for a young woman of your social status to have continued without the company of a chaperone."

My fumbling efforts just irritated her even more. "I will admit to no such thing. I can take care of myself, Ranger Dodge. At the age of six I fought Comanches beside my father on our ranch west of Waco."

"Be that as it may, you didn't do very well in this instance." Boz tried to soften the truth of the matter as much as he could. She let the gentle slap pass and went back to her victuals.

"Did he make unseemly advances?" Had no enthusiasm for hitting her with that particular question, but figured if I didn't, Boz would.

"He did not, sir," she snapped. "Morgan Tingwell was a perfect gentleman, despite the fact that we traveled with no other company for the last fifty miles before reaching Iron Bluff."

"Well, then, how did you end up wherever you've been

for the past month?" Boz was beginning to get impatient and you could hear it in his voice.

"While a perfect gentleman on the stagecoach, I must admit Mr. Tingwell lied like a yellow dog. The stage makes an overnight stop at the hotel here in town. He invited me to spend that time at his family estate, and assured me his mother and sisters would see to my every comfort."

I couldn't help but snicker. "He called that nightmare a family estate?"

She stopped fiddling with the food, stared at her hands, and twisted the front of her dress into a knot. "Yes. But I had no reason to disbelieve him. When we met, he'd been to New Orleans on business." She got kind of flustered and blurted, "He was well dressed and displayed perfect manners, I can assure you. I would not have gone with him otherwise."

Boz glanced at me. "Hard to believe the Morgan Tingwell we're familiar with is the same man—very hard to believe."

A heavy sigh escaped before she could hold it back. "Well, he proved totally undependable. Mr. Tingwell rented a hack from the local smith. When we arrived at that outlandish hodgepodge he called an estate, gentlemen, I must admit, I almost passed out. Before I could do anything to save myself, he grabbed me by the wrist and dragged me inside his clan's hideous cave of a dwelling."

"His parents didn't do anything to help you?"

My question drew a sharp-eyed look that should have taken my head off. She snapped, "As soon as we got past the front door, he announced to the entire witless tribe that he'd found the woman of his dreams and would keep me in spite of hell, high water, or any objections they might harbor. Said he planned to make me his wife and have children as soon as possible. My God, his impudence knew no limit. And worse, his idiot parents were pleased as punch."

Boz tried to calm her with what I felt was an easy question, but perhaps the most important of all. "Did the Tingwells cause you any bodily harm?"

"No, my good sir. No one laid an unkind finger on me." She sounded tired when she said it.

Her answer surprised me a bit. So I got a tad more forceful. "Then how did they manage to ensure your captivity?"

Took a spell before I got an answer to that one. Finally she looked up at me and said, "Morgan's mother and three sisters watched me day and night. One of them slept near me in a dungeonlike room the entire time they held me. The outside of their home is hideous, but can't hold a candle to the inside. Put me in mind of a realistic description of hell on earth. It wasn't what they did, so much, as what they implied would happen if I tried to escape."

"How's that, Miss Ruby?" I asked.

"Well, as an example, the day you came to the ranch, I watched the entire scene from inside. Mother Tingwell told me if I cried out, her boys would kill both of you. Morgan's sisters took turns reinforcing her warning."

Boz pushed it even harder. "Was that the first time they threatened you?"

"Sweet Merciful Father, no. I'd heard similar words of coercion, two or three times a day, since my arrival. That particular threat didn't involve any physical harm to me, but would have left the painful weight of your deaths on my heart, until the moment of my own passing. I could not cast dice with your lives and cry out, for fear they would make good on the threat."

Boz stood, pushed his chair away from the desk, and said, "I've listened to enough of this for one day. Don't know if there's anything we can do unless you want to press charges against them for false imprisonment. Given where we are, though, any legal action you take might be hard to make stick, since you went with Morgan and didn't attempt to escape. Doesn't sound too good, does it?"

Her chin dropped to her chest. "Yes, Ranger Tatum. I see exactly what you mean." Then her head snapped up and she said, "I would prefer that what transpired regarding the Tingwells and me never see the light of day. Courtrooms, trials, and newspaper headlines are not something I want in my future. Such events would be an agonizing embarrassment to my family."

Boz threw me a knowing glance and nodded. "It will be as you request, Miss Ruby," I said.

She stood and rubbed her hands together as though pleased. "Good. Ranger Dodge, I've been inside now for much too long and would fancy a nice walk to settle my meal. Would you be willing to accompany me on a brief sashay around town?"

Boz smiled and bowed his head. "You two go right ahead. I'll stay here and keep an eye on things. But be watchful, Lucius. Don't trust them Tingwells any further than I can throw my horse—especially one as woman-hungry as Morgan."

She took my arm once we got outside. Her lilac perfume crept up my arm, assaulted the edges of my nose, and turned my head so I could get a better look at her in the flickering streetlight. My God, don't think I'd ever seen anything more beautiful. Seemed to me as though she'd been reborn. The smile on her face, as we strolled past the Fin and Feather, barbershop, bank, wagon yard, and tailor shop, grew with each step.

At the end of the street she pulled me to the other side and toward the town's empty church. She said, "I'd like to pay a visit, if you don't mind, Ranger Dodge."

"Of course, Miss Black, but I doubt the preacher is available this late. Probably at home having supper by now."

"Doesn't matter. My needs involve a talk with God. A preacher would simply prove an unwanted distraction. You may watch from the back pew," she said as we pushed the door open.

It took a few moments for our eyes to adjust to the deeper darkness. "Would you like me to light a lamp?"

"No. Prayers work just as well in the dark. Besides, I'm not entirely sure I want God to see my face while we talk tonight. Do you understand, Ranger Dodge?"

"Please call me Lucius, Miss Black. Don't think anyone would mind while we're in church."

"Only if you can promise to stop calling me Miss, One Thing or Another. Can you do that?"

"Yes, Ruby, pretty sure I can."

She left me at the door and strode directly to the rough altar below the minister's raised podium. A wooden cross, all of three feet high, decorated the stand. She knelt before that crooked tree, placed one hand on it, and covered her face with the other. I couldn't hear what Ruby said to God that night. Her whispered prayers and tearful beseeching made their way to me as little more than garbled, but sincere, words from a soul relieved of great distress.

She went at her devotions so long, I finally took a seat. But my rump had barely hit the pew when she hurried back to the door and was ready to leave. On the street, I could detect tears in the corners of her eyes and offered my kerchief.

She dabbed at the dampness, held tighter to my arm, and said, "I'm just so thankful to be away from those horrid people. Honestly, I thought you'd never come, Lucius. But the day the Tingwells made me watch from their house and threatened to kill you, I knew things were about to change dramatically. There you were—the answer to all my most heartfelt prayers. Loaded down with pistols and decorated in twinkling silver. I knew, when you rode up on your big blue horse, things would get better fast. How could they not? I've never known a man who sparkled like that and rode a blue horse."

"He's a blue roan, Ruby."

"A mere detail, Lucius, a mere detail. The only thing that could have made your arrival any better would have been if you had shown up riding a white horse and wearing a suit of armor." She tightened her grip on my arm. First time in my life I felt like a hero, and a girl I barely knew did it.

We strolled along the boardwalk on the west side of town past the doctor's office and pharmacy, telegraph, hardware emporium and mercantile, hotel, the Matador Saloon, and Hermione's café. I'd started us back across the street to the jail, but she stopped me in the darkened alleyway between the café and a laundry run by a Chinese family. Twirled me around on my heel and kissed me so hard my spurs went to spinning so fast I thought I'd fly. And you know, there for two or three seconds no one living could've made me believe that stunningly beautiful girl and me didn't fly some.

She broke the kiss, skittered away to the jail door, and disappeared inside. Left me standing in the dark, shaking like a windblown leaf during a Texas twister. I couldn't help but smile. Thought to myself, Lucius, that red-haired gal just made you love her more than anything living—and all she used was one kiss.

Next morning, I still floated on a cloud of unbridled need when she came to breakfast and made my situation even worse by simply smiling at me again. Those feelings didn't last long, though. Only got to enjoy them for about five minutes. That's when Quincy Beakins knocked on the door and ruined my whole day.

Boz yelled, "Come on in."

Door opened wide enough for a man's hatless head to appear. "I'm lookin' for Marshal Stonehill."

"He's out of town at the moment." I said. "Don't know when he'll return. Could we help you?"

"Are you fellers lawmen?"

"Texas Rangers," Boz said. "Good enough for you?"

"I reckon you'll have to do." With some obvious hesitation, our visitor made his way inside and carefully closed the door. He held a badly abused gray felt hat in both hands, twisted it back and forth between rough, gnarled fingers. Dressed in a leather vest, cotton shirt, heavy canvas pants, and well-used boots, he gave the appearance of a man who most likely worked a small cattle operation.

"Name's Quincy Beakins. Run some cows 'bout a mile north of town over near the Angelina. Went out looking for strays early this morning. Found some fellers hanging in a tree. Think maybe somebody done went and lynched 'em."

Boz and I pushed away from the table and jumped for our weapons. As we got ourselves armed, my partner said, "How many fellers, Mr. Beakins?"

"Two. Local cowboys, I believe. Think I recognized one of 'em. My pissant operation borders the Tingwell place, and the one poor brush-popper looked a lot like a Tingwell rider named Ford Fargo. Course identification proved a mite hard, bein' as how his face was all swolled up and discolorated like it was."

"You search either man?" I asked.

"Hell, no. Ain't nobody gonna catch me goin' through the pockets of no corpses."

Beakins and Boz headed for the door. Boz said, "I'll saddle the horses, Lucius. You make sure Ruby's situated before we leave."

I'd barely got turned around good when she fell on my

chest like Beakins had announced the end of the world. She held me tight and said, "I know you have to go. Please be careful. The Tingwells are far more dangerous than they appear. Should anything happen to you, I'm not sure I could bear it."

Tilted her chin up with my finger, gently kissed her, and said, "Don't worry, Ruby. I'll be fine." Pushed myself away and went to the gun rack. "I've loaded the shotgun, two of the rifles, and a pistol. Keep the door locked. Don't let anyone in. Hermione brings our meals, and will leave them outside if she knocks and no one answers. Should Morgan Tingwell show his ugly face, shoot through the door. We'll be back as soon as possible. Do you understand?"

"Yes, Lucius. Don't worry. I can take care of myself now."

As I headed for the door, she grabbed my hand, pulled it to her face, and kissed my palm. Made me weak in the knees and fanned a desire to stay with her rather than leave. But I had to go.

I waited outside till she'd forced the bolt on the door. Boz had the horses ready. Jumped into my saddle, and we followed Quincy. He led us out the same road we'd taken to the Tingwell ranch, but turned onto a barely detectable cow path little over a mile outside town.

Couldn't have taken more than half an hour to find those poor bastards. Beakins led us through the dense woods and into a clearing right at the edge of the river. He reined up, then pointed to a spot less than a hundred yards farther up. To say the site was shocking doesn't come close to a description of what we saw. There's just something about finding a dead man that can make your skin crawl. Can't imagine the impact on Beakins when he came on two of them all alone.

Hazy sunlight cut through a mixed stand of blackjack

oak, hickory, pine, and cottonwoods. Stringy clouds raced overhead against a sky of such bright liquid blue it hurt to look at it.

At the edge of that bare opening in the woodlands, a single cottonwood that must have stood there thirty or forty years split about ten feet from the base and formed two enormous trunks. The closest limbs to the ground were as big around as my arm, extended over a patch of deep green grass, and sported a pair of horrific decorations.

"There they be, Rangers. Fargo's the one hanging from the limb on the left. Cain't say who t'other one was. All the same to you boys, I'll leave you here and get on back to my family. My wife's scared slap to death over all this. Besides, I ain't got no desire to look on them poor dead waddies again, lest you insist."

Boz spurred his horse and didn't look back as he called over his shoulder, "You go to your family, Mr. Beakins. We'll take care of 'em."

First time I'd ever seen anyone lynched was that day on the banks of the Angelina. I'd been to a few legal hangings, but never one done by amateurs. Some major differences existed between the two brands of execution. Court-ordered hangings tended to be done by men who made their living at it. The condemned usually died quickly of a broken neck. Not so with the vigilante brand of oak tree justice. The old saw about "havin' your neck stretched" proved an absolute truism in such killings.

With a goodly measure of trepidation, Boz and me rode over to the ghastly sight. Immediately understood why Beakins didn't want to stick around for another viewing. Poor cow-chaser he called Ford Fargo looked like his head was a foot from his body and twisted sharply over onto one shoulder. A black tongue, the size of my hand, lolled out the side of his mouth. Blank eyes stared into space. An appearance of pained torment was etched in deep lines across his contorted visage. Worst of all, the cottonwood limb the dead man swung from had drooped so much his toes touched the ground, and he almost appeared to be standing.

Boz's chin dropped to his chest. When he finally looked up again he said, "God Almighty, what a horrible way to go out of this life. Ain't no one deserves to choke to death tip-toeing at the end of a rope."

I spurred Grizz up closer to the second corpse. Unknown buckaroo seemed to have had a better time of it than his friend. His rope had been dropped over a stouter limb and, on the surface of it at least, dead man looked as though he'd gone out pretty quick. But the sombrero-sized pool of blood at his feet belied that conclusion.

Once we got him down, Boz pulled the dead man's shirt back and said, "Whoever strung him up couldn't wait around for this feller to die. They shot the hell out of him. Eight holes in his chest."

I said, "Well, guess you hit the nail on the head this time, Boz. You said the Pitts would have their revenge where no witness could see what happened. Be willing to bet Nick Fox and Alvin Clements caught these poor goobers out here alone and strung 'em up. Hell, I'd be prepared to place an even bigger bet Clements rode straight from his jail cell, found some help, and lynched these poor boys within an hour of us releasing him."

"Could be, Lucius, but we'll never know for sure, unless someone comes forward and admits to the deed."

We'd got ourselves in such a rush, neither of us thought to bring pack animals. Had to throw them poor deceased leather-pounders over the backs of our own horses and walk them into town. Found Iron Bluff's undertaker, man named Tyrone Pinkus, and dropped them off with him.

Pinkus said, "I'll do what I can to make 'em a bit more presentable. Not sure there's much help for this 'un with the stretched neck. Get 'em in the ground soon as possible. Tomorrow afternoon, if I can find me a grave digger. Don't suppose it's gonna matter much how they look anyway. Be surprised if anyone turns up for the interment."

Well, Pinkus missed the mark on his assessment of the situation. Next day around two o'clock, when those poor dead boys went in the ground, the entire Tingwell crew stormed into town and set up shop in the Matador. Don't know to this minute exactly how they found out about the funeral, but news of two murders does travel fast in small towns.

Tingwell's boys were madder than hell, and less than an hour after they arrived, drunk enough to cause trouble. Every one of them made it to the church service, and later to the graveyard. Think damn near all those men came away from the ceremony red-eyed and ready to kill somebody else.

Boz and I watched from our chairs, in front of the jail, as the whole gang raged back from the cemetery. They yelled, and cussed, everyone in sight. Tried to pick fights with some of the townspeople. Generally made jackasses out of themselves.

Boz said, "Let 'em drink, yell, and holler. Long as they don't do anything more, I'm willing to look the other way."

Seemed a fine idea to me, leastways until Romulus Pitt and his crowd rode into town and headed for the Fin and Feather. Personally couldn't think of another way the arrogant son of a bitch might have been more provocative than storming into town leading the pack of killers who were most likely responsible for the Tingwell band's grief.

Soon as Pitt thundered past us, tied up, and stomped into his private cow-country oasis, Boz moaned and then said, "God Almighty. We've got real trouble now." He stood, rearranged his pistol belt, and grabbed the shotgun. "Get ready, Lucius. Looks to me like this is gonna be a bad day in Iron Bluff. If we ain't ankle deep in blood before mornin', I'll be shocked and amazed."

But a funny thing happened that afternoon. For all the yelling, mean-mouthing, and colorful language thrown back and forth, from either side of the street, nothing happened. Leastways, not until Boz and me had begun to breathe a bit easier and fool ourselves into thinking that maybe we'd managed to get luckier than the gambler who drew six pat hands in a row.

Hell, Ruby had just stepped outside, with a pail of cool water and a dipper for us, when we heard the shots. Came from down on the end of the street near the church.

I turned to Ruby and said, "Get inside and bar the door. Don't come out till I get back. Think the serious killing Boz talked about might well have started."

10

"Won't Be Nothin' Left of Your Head but the Stalk of Bone It Sits On"

RUBY DISAPPEARED LIKE a beautiful magician's assistant, there one second covered with a giant silk scarf, then gone the next. Boz hit the street running before echoes from the first two or three blasts had stopped ricocheting down the street. I couldn't have been more than ten steps behind him, but couldn't catch up.

Heavy wall of gunfire came from behind a fence that ran along the street between Iron Bluff's Baptist church and the Ransom brothers' stable and smith operation. The blood-soaked bodies of two men were sprawled in the middle of the street. One of them had a dead sorrel partially atop him. The other feller's animal must have been hit too. It flew past me slinging black blood from its nose. Poor beast screamed in pain like one of hell's most tormented souls. Made the hair on back of my neck stand. Got an odd prickly sensation up and down my spine. Whining bullets still peppered both men, even though it was obvious one feller appeared totally dead and the other was on the way.

I saw Boz drop to his knees behind the lifeless hay burner and send both barrels of buckshot at the fence. Dirt and wood splinters flew in every direction like drunken flies feeding on a bloated carcass. One of the shooters hidden behind the fence yelped like a kicked dog. A cloud of flying dust, gun smoke, blood, and death still hung in the heavy air.

My partner dropped the shotgun, pulled both pistols, and pumped hot lead into the spot he'd just peppered. I dropped beside him, and levered shells through the Winchester as fast as I could pump them out. Some poor clueless folks, who'd been in the church for an evening service, poured out the front door and went to running, yelling, and screaming. Distraction caused me to look back toward the jail. Boardwalks in front of both saloons teemed with drunken cowboys and gunfighters.

"Jesus, Boz. Looks like Tingwell and Pitt are about to open the ball on an all-out war," I yelled.

He stopped pitching lead long enough for us to hear horses gallop away from a spot behind the church. I followed Boz when he headed for the fence. Jumped over and made it around the corner in time to see two men kicking hard in the direction of the Angelina. We ripped off a few more shots. Didn't appear to have done any useful damage.

Boz ejected all his empties and reloaded as we ran back to the street to retrieve his shotgun. Once we got ourselves fully primed and charged again, he said, "Damn. This looks bad. Tell you what, Lucius, we'll come back to these poor boys later. Ain't nothin' much we can do for 'em now anyways. Best see to those left alive before they do anything stupid."

"Sounds like a good plan to me, Boz."

"Gonna be a shade touchy. Watch my back. I'll do the

talkin'. Shoot the hell out of any man who makes a move for his pistol, son."

Pitt, Fox, and Clements led a boiling mob that was moving our direction. Drunken rabble was almost nose to nose with Tingwell, Hatch, and Casper Longstreet. I heard Boz mumble, "Jesus, them bushwhackin' bastards lit the fuse for damned sure. We've gotta snuff this out right now, Lucius."

By the time we got to the heavily armed swarm of men, they'd managed to argue their way to a spot in the middle of the street between the hardware store, on one side of the dusty thoroughfare, and the barbershop, on the other.

About the moment we ran up, I saw Pitt shake a knotted finger in Bull Tingwell's face and scream, "You sent them to kill my men, you half-witted, sheep-loving, tater-digging son of a bitch, but it didn't work did it?"

Tingwell didn't even flinch. Fox and Clements had death in their eyes. John Roman Hatch looked calmer than water in a horse trough during a drought, and Longstreet's pallor had gone from death to something like been-in-the-ground-for-a-week. Before I could spit, Pitt's sons ran into the street behind their father. Fact is, everyone showed up, except Morgan Tingwell. Thought it odd he didn't put in an appearance.

Boz pulled a trick so bold I still get chill bumps just thinking about it. The various potential combatants were so consumed in their individual anger, and hatred, none of them even noticed us, till we'd walked right up in the middle of the situation. Boz slipped the muzzle of his coach gun under Romulus Pitt's chin with one hand, then pulled a pistol with the other and pointed it at Bull Tingwell's crotch. Didn't take much guidance to give me the hint. I strolled over, pressed my rifle barrel to Tingwell's temple, and waited. God Almighty, but everything got quieter than a tree full of owls.

Don't know if anyone else noticed it, but Boz was wound

up tighter than a banjo string when he said, "Tell your men to ride out, Pitt. Do it now. Same goes for you, Tingwell."

Pitt snorted, "You've lost your mind, Tatum. My men will cut you to ribbons. All I have to do is give the word."

So low I could barely hear him, Boz said, "Go ahead. Give the word. But know this. Soon as you open your mouth there won't be nothin' left of your head but the stalk of bone it sits on."

Pitt's eyes got the size of twenty-dollar gold pieces. Calmly as possible, I added, "My partner's not real stable right now, gents. If I were you, I'd do what he says. Bull, you'd best tell your clan to hotfoot it back to the ranch. The Texas Rangers will sort this out. Take care of whoever is responsible. Understand?"

Hardy Tingwell carefully pushed his plainsman's hat to the back of his head and said, "Guess we've got something of a standoff goin' here, don't we, Rangers?"

Boz let a strangled chuckle escape. I glanced at Hardy and said, "No. No standoff. If anything goes amiss, Hardy, my first shot will blow most of your old man's brains all over your bib-front shirt, and the second is guaranteed to send you to God on an outhouse door."

Bull Tingwell raised his left hand and gestured for his volatile son to shut his stupid mouth. The old man said, "Get our boys out of town right now, Hardy. Point 'em for the ranch. Don't look back. These two men don't talk just to hear their heads rattle. They'll kill me, sure as Hell's hot. Go on, git, boy."

"Not till Pitt sends his men packin' too, Pa." Had to hand it to the crazier of old man Tingwell's idiot sons. He'd grown a small piece of brain somewhere along the road.

Pitt turned to Nick Fox. "You and Clements get everyone back to the ranch. Don't cause any trouble between here and there. That's an order, you hear me? Do it now."

You'd of had to be deaf and stupid not to get his point. Underneath what he was barely able to whisper was a simple message. "Don't do anything dim-witted. If you do, Tingwell and I are dead men for sure."

Took almost ten minutes for all those angry cowboys to get saddled up and on the move. Tingwell's bunch fogged out of town first. Their quickness didn't sit well with Fox and Clements. The two hired killers rode up to the spot where we still had both family leaders under the gun.

Fox yelled, "If we get ambushed on the way out of town, I'll come back here and kill both you Ranger sons of bitches like yeller dogs."

Once the fuming clans vacated the street and headed north, the situation leveled out a mite. Guess nothing out of the way occurred. Both groups must've gone their separate ways without incident.

Boz let the hammers down on his shotgun. I followed my partner's lead. Pitt pulled his hat off, and wiped an ocean of sweat from saturated hair. Old Man Tingwell didn't act like he'd been bothered in the least. We'd barely managed to feel a degree of relief when a series of shocking rifle blasts, from near the jail, rocked us again.

Boz led the way back past the Fin and Feather. The rest of us followed fast as we could hoof it. Stretched out, about ten feet from the front door of the jail, Morgan Tingwell flopped around like a beached carp. Ruby stood on the porch, jacked another shell into a Yellow Boy Winchester, and popped him again. Think that one probably put an end to him. Got him just above the right eye, and ripped off most of his head.

I ran to Ruby and snatched the rifle out of her hand. Girl's eyes were glazed over like she was in some kind of a trance, or something. Bull Tingwell headed for his blood-soaked son. Ole Bull fell to his knees in the dusty street and started howling like the only wolf left in the great cold and lonely.

Pitt stopped near the corner of the saloon, and didn't seem inclined to come any closer. Personally couldn't blame him. Way I had it figured, Tingwell would probably find some way to point the finger at the elder Pitt for the stupid, lust-driven Morgan's death. That would naturally lead to another gory shooting.

Boz bent over the boy's lifeless body, glanced up at me, and shook his head. A still-blubbering Bull Tingwell jumped to wobbly feet. Boz whipped his shotgun barrel around and knocked the pistol out of the old geezer's hand. Tingwell yelped like a whipped dog and started for Ruby.

I stepped in front of the shaking girl. Leveled my rifle up at Tingwell's middle. He stopped, pointed a trembling finger at Ruby, and yelled, "I saved you, goddamnit. Brought you to these men. This is how you repay me?"

Ruby pushed me aside and screamed, "You and your family kept me captive for more than a month. You did nothing, until Lucius and Boz forced the issue. If you'd taken the proper steps in the first place, none of this would have happened."

Bull tried his best to get at Ruby. Boz held him off, while I tried to stay between them. Bull kept yelling, "You killed my son, you whoring bitch."

Under my arm Ruby shouted, "He tried to break into the jail. You told him where I was, didn't you, old man? It's your fault."

Her unexpected revelation stopped Bull's mindless ranting. Rooted him to the ground like a frozen tree in a blue norther. He tried to speak again, but nothing understandable came out.

Boz said, "Take your son and go home, Mr. Tingewll. We told Miss Black to defend herself should anyone unauthorized try to enter the jail during our absence. Morgan had no business here and, from the appearance of our front door, he must have attempted to force his way in with a pry bar of some kind." Boz searched along the ground to his right and pointed. "Yes, there, by the hitch rack. He probably dropped it when the first shot hit him."

Tingwell shook as if in the throes of some hideous East Texas swamp fever. He turned, and in a voice that sounded like it came from the bottom of a newly opened grave, said to Boz, "I hold you Rangers responsible for my boy's murder, Tatum. My son's dead because of you. I'll have your blood in return and, by God, I'll take your lives any way I can get them." Then, he whipped back around on Ruby and hissed, "If there's a God in heaven, you'll die alongside them, you black-hearted bitch."

Romulus Pitt got himself horsed and headed out of town as fast as good animal flesh could run. Boz and I both figured he couldn't wait to get back to his ranch and have a good laugh over all the Tingwell men his clan had left in Iron Bluff's street.

Boz offered to take the dead men to the undertaker's, but the elder Tingwell refused. "I'll bury my son on the ranch. Don't want him in no town cemetery. These others was fine young men. Neither of them ever so much as hurt a fly. I feel obligated to take care of 'em. Besides, I don't want you bastards doin' nuthin' for me. Get the hell out of my way." The old man loaded up his dead son, and the two other cowboys, and led them away.

We moved aside, stood on the jail's little porch, and watched ole Bull leave town. Once he'd disappeared from view, I turned to the door and examined the damage Morgan had left behind. Noticed several bullet holes near the knob.

"Ruby, did Morgan fire into the door?" I asked.

"Yes. He pried on it for some time. I kept pleading with

him to stop, but he wouldn't. Then, he gave up on the crowbar and started blasting at the knob. That's when I fired back. You can see where I shot through the door at him, up here near the peep slot."

Sure enough, a single hole, about shoulder high, had exited exactly where she indicated. I picked at the splinters and said, "But you opened the door and shot him at least two more times, didn't you."

Her chin dropped to her chest. We could barely hear her say, "Yes. And by God, I'd do it again. Worthless scum didn't deserve to live."

Boz pushed us both inside, and slammed the bolt on the door. Ruby fell into a chair, leaned forward with her head in her hands, and wept. I tried to comfort her, but didn't do much good. Reassurance usually proves about as worthless as speaking Chinese to a Texas mustang when you've just finished killing a man the way she'd killed Morgan Tingwell. But for the life of me, I still can't imagine why she got so upset. Hell, she'd said it herself. He deserved to die. His passing at my hand, or Boz's, wouldn't have bothered either of us much, but Ruby suffered over the act for quite a spell.

Boz threw his hat on the desk, ran the fingers of both hands through his hair, and said, "Well, Lucius, we've got one hell of a mess on our hands. Have to admit I never expected so much death in such a short time. Looks to me like we're gonna have the war we've been expecting on our hands right damned quick. These back-and-forth shootings, hangings, and such are sure to break out into the open shortly. I think Bull's good for his word. We'd best keep a weather eye on our backs from now on."

Tried to be optimistic when I said, "Maybe we can still keep the lid on this jug sealed. You know, make sure they stay out of town. Do their killing somewhere else."

"I doubt it." Boz shook his head, pulled a six-inch bowie from his boot, and picked at his fingernails. "Worst part of the whole dance is there probably ain't time enough to get any Ranger reinforcements in here to help us out. Take a week, or ten days, to bring in a full contingent of Rangers to put this thing down, even longer for the state to send in the militia. Think we're in this one alone."

But he was wrong about that. Next morning, Rip Thorn made it back to town. Got to admit, I felt one hell of a lot better when that bear-sized man showed up.

11

"DONE COME TO KILL YOU BOYS"

"DAMN, YOU MEAN I chased Judge Stanley Cooper all over hell and yonder for nothing?" Rip stood in the middle of the office holding the court order in his hand like a pet bird that had died.

I said, "Sorry, Rip. Situation worked itself out about as well as we could have wished—at least as far as Ruby is concerned."

"What do you mean by 'as far as Ruby is concerned'?" The big man's neck and face colored up, and there, for a minute, I thought he just might be on the verge of losing his temper.

I said, "Well, Bull Tingwell helped us get Ruby back. Unfortunately, we've had an uncommon number of killings done by both sides since you left. Looks to me as though our worst fears concerning this whole situation are about to come to a fiery peak. We're pretty sure it was members of the Pitt bunch that waylayed two of Tingwell's men yesterday evening, right in the middle of Main Street."

Boz added, "And even worse than all of that, but wonderful news for us, Ruby shot hell out of Morgan Tingwell when he tried to break into the jail and steal her back. Ole Bull is not a happy man today. Figure he's got men digging three graves out on his ranch."

Rip threw Judge Cooper's stamped, sealed, and signed document on the desk and said, "Well, hell, you boys have been busy since I left, haven't you."

At the same instant, Boz and I both said, "That ain't the half of it."

Took us several more minutes to fill Thorn in on the entire story since his departure for San Augustine. All he could do was shake his massive head and look thoughtful.

When we'd finished dropping as much bad news on the man as we could remember, he said, "Well, don't sound like no Sunday picnic coming our way. Be damned lucky if both tribes don't ride into town and shoot hell out of everything they can see, including us."

Boz said, "Think we'd best stick close to the jail, boys. Figure we'll be safer here than anywhere else—for a few days at least. I wouldn't want to get caught out in the briars and brambles north of town with men being lynched and ambushed right and left the way they are. Gonna have to keep alert, even while here in town."

Way it all fell out, Boz set up a patrol schedule that kept at least two of us on the street, from daybreak till midnight, while one man stayed in the jail with Ruby. He rotated the plan around in such a manner as to give me a chance to spend more time with the girl, and the arrangement worked pretty well, for the first day or two. By then, Ruby'd had all of Marshal Stonehill's lockup a body could stand. Decided she wanted to go on a picnic. Boz didn't cotton to the idea a bit and tried his best to discourage her, but Ruby pleaded. Girl could be right persuasive when she wanted.

Hermione Blackstock prepared a nice basket for us. We headed out toward Lone Pine in search of a suitable spot. Boz insisted we stay to the south. Figured it would be safer.

Found a shady cove on the banks of the Angelina a few miles out of town. Fast-moving water spilled over moss-covered rocks and helped cool the surrounding area considerably. Patches of red, yellow, blue, and purple wildflowers grew in shaded spots along both banks, and scented the heavy air with a perfume that delighted my beautiful companion.

I threw down a blanket. Ruby got the thick ham sandwiches, pickled eggs, and other items Hermonie fixed for us arranged to her satisfaction. We settled in for a pleasant afternoon.

The girl's strange captivity had started to fade into memory. I noticed as how she'd finally begun to assume the personality of a spirited, unattached young woman again. Ruby Black was one hell of a flirt too, and knew exactly how to make an interested man get flushed, fill his britches full of sweat, and squirm.

She glanced up from a checkerboard we'd brought along, gave me one of those "Aren't-I-just-the-most-beautiful-thing-you've-ever-seen" looks, and said, "Do you have a lady friend in Fort Worth, Lucius?"

"Lady friend?"

"Yes. You know what I mean. Some young lady you're courting."

"Courting?"

"I hadn't noticed that you answer questions with more questions until now."

'Bout then I realized I probably sounded like an idiot, but couldn't help myself—typical man-in-the-company-of-an-overpowering-female-presence kind of thing. Encounters for us, in and around the jail, had been seriously constricted by the close proximity of Boz, or someone else, during the entire time of our acquaintance. The only exception had been the walk she'd insisted we take to the church. Now, here we were totally alone, and my brain had turned to mush and detached itself from my mouth.

With some degree of personal embarrassment, I stared into her eyes said, "There is no woman, young or old, in my life, Ruby. Me and Boz spend too much time running evil people to ground. As a consequence, I'm not sure any lady of breeding, or refinement, would want to waste time allowing a man like me to bestow my sporadic attentions on her."

Ruby's full, rouged lips parted in a coquettish smile. She tilted her head and said, "You're wrong, Lucius. There are plenty of girls who'd be thrilled to know a handsome gentleman possessed of such outstanding qualities as yours might be interested in them." She let the obvious compliment lie between us for a beat or two, then added, "Know for certain I would."

Her open, and extremely bold, invitation took me by surprise. But when she leaned forward and kissed me, in much the same manner she had the night of our walk to the church, it became crystal clear that Ruby Black was more than a *little* interested. The heat from that first kiss had stayed with me, right up till the moment of the second one there on the banks of the Angelina.

Somewhere deep inside my thundering heart, I knew I should have pushed her away and pointed out such conduct didn't become ladies of sophistication. I thought to myself that passionate kisses between two people who barely knew

one another must surely have violated the rules of gentle-
manly conduct, in some manner or other.

But chivalrous behavior was a thing foreign to an ill-
educated ruffian such as myself. So I kissed her back. Hell,
I kissed her till we both almost exploded with desire. Fifteen or twenty minutes into the thing, her lips were swollen,
her cheeks reddened by my poor efforts at shaving. I think
she would have continued for as long, and gone as far, as I
would have wanted to go with my amorous advances.

After an extended bout of boldly ardent conduct, on both
our parts, unforeseen gallantry did rear its ugly head, in spite
of all I could do to fight it off. Wrestled my most wicked
cravings down, and pushed the still-passionate girl to arm's
length. No display of pained disappointment appeared on
her face. On the contrary, she looked most pleased that I'd
taken the initiative and stopped our enthusiastic grappling
match, before we'd gone too far to turn back.

She smiled again, traced my lower lip with her thumb,
and said, "There's plenty of time, dear Lucius. Perhaps a
lifetime."

The rest of our starry-eyed afternoon by the Angelina
exists in my memory as a bewilderment of the mind—a
kind of dreamlike recollection that comes to me as if
viewed underwater, through a piece of cut glass. Somehow
we got back to town, but any detailed recollection of the
return on my part would be pure conjecture. Like a mis-
chievous red-haired sprite, Ruby had bewitched me, and
the spell that stunning girl cast left me in a state of profound happiness.

The passionate reservoir of overheated lightheadedness
I felt when in her presence got pushed aside two days later.
Rip and I walked our usual patrol that evening. A molten
sun dipped low on the horizon and fried the earth to sizzling. Everyone we met expressed a degree of near-cosmic

satisfaction that the temperature would soon drop to something approximating a bearable, but still sweat-saturated, level.

Horace Breedlove took a moment from sweeping the boardwalk in front of his store to make small talk as we passed. "Hotter'n a burning stump, ain't it, Rangers?"

Rip winked at me and said, "Hell, Horace, it's so hot I done heard as how a farmer out toward Lone Pine is havin' to feed his chickens cracked ice to keep 'em from laying hard-boiled eggs."

In the spirit of undeclared competition, and not to be outdone, Breedlove shot back, "That a fact? Have to admit I was not aware of such singular marvels. I can testify, however, that one of my customers showed me a rash of blisters that popped out on his pistol belt. Man said he was absolutely certain they were a direct result of this month-long crush of heat we've suffered. Sold him a can of Morton's Prickly Heat Powder to treat the problem."

Rip threw his head back and laughed. "He must've been over San Augustine way for a few days. When I visited there, a week or so back, potatoes was bakin' in the ground."

I grabbed Rip by the arm and pulled him away. Said, "That's enough. Bet you two could go on for hours with this meadow muffin-pitching contest."

He and the shopkeeper laughed even harder as Rip shouted over his shoulder, "Sorry, Horace, didn't even get to mention as how all the corn in Gonzales County's done went and popped off the stalk."

We stumbled into the middle of the street, giggled like kids, and were headed for the church when Hardy Tingwell just kind of appeared, about forty feet in front of us, as though he'd suddenly burst out of the ground like a fast-growing stalk of stinkweed. Meanest Tingwell alive swaggered toward us, both hands clasped around the walnut butts of his pistols.

"Done come to kill you boys," he shouted.

"Who the hell's this?" Rip whispered.

I said, "Tingwell's only remaining son, Hardy. Think you might have seen him briefly when we visited their ranch. From what I've heard, he's two shades meaner than the devil, and deadly with those Colts."

Thought at first the boy had to be drunker than Cooter Brown to brace the two of us in such a manner. In less than a heartbeat, it became patently obvious that he was stone-cold sober, looking to do murder. His solemn clearheaded-ness contributed to a situation that was even more dangerous than I'd first believed.

Rip tried some soft-glove diplomacy when he said, "Think you have the advantage on me, mister. Name's Rip Thorn. Who might you be?"

"Your murderin' friend knows who I am, you enormous gob of greasy spit. But just so you'll understand who kilt you, my name's Hardy Tingwell, you son of a bitch. Been waitin' to open court on you bastards for almost an hour. Done found all you Ranger jackasses guilty of the foul murder of my brother Morgan, and aim to carry out sen-tence right here, right by-God now. Death, that's what I says. Death to all of you."

Made what I thought was a calming motion with my hand and said, "Need to cool off, Hardy. Neither of us had anything to do with your brother's passing. Fact is, he brought about his own departure from this earth with some amazingly stupid behavior."

Tingwell's upper lip peeled back in a toothless sneer as he shouted, "That's a black damnable lie, and you know it. If 'n you boys hadn't showed up looking for that red-haired whore, Morgan would still be alive. Gonna have to 'fess up to your sins, Dodge."

Rip said, "Your brother stole the lady. Imprisoned her again her will. If she hadn't protected herself, he would most likely have swung for what he done. Know if I had anything to say about it, he'd a been broke-necked and purple-tongued long before she had a chance to shoot him."

"Piss on you, you egg-suckin' dog. Slab-sided pork butts like you make damned fine targets, Ranger. Gonna take great pleasure blasting craters in your lard ass."

Personally felt ole Hardy had signed his own death warrant when he called Ruby a whore. Stood and waited for him to make a move with his pistols, so I could blast the hell out of him. Knew the first move would come when his eyes narrowed just a bit, but the setting sun made it a mite hard for me to see his eyes very well. Was in the process of figuring I'd have to depend on something else for a tell, when he jerked both his monstrous Smith and Wesson pistols.

"Damn you—and all those like you," he screamed.

Felt hot lead chew a hole in the air near my left ear. Heard at least one round make a strange thumping noise from Rip's direction. Had my belly pistol out faster than double-greased lightning. Ripped off as many shots as I could before I had to get my hip gun into play as well.

Hardy yelled, "I'll kill the hell out of both you sons of bitches. Gonna string your guts on fence rails."

Snaggle-toothed nitwit might have had all the brains of a flour sifter, but he'd been smart enough to start the fiery dance from a fairly safe distance. It's always been my experience, if you're in a hurry and under considerable duress, pistol fighting at more than ten paces is a fairly iffy proposition. Surest way to kill a man in such a contest is to be as close as possible, take your time, aim, and blast the offending party out of his boots. Better yet, carry a rifle or a shotgun. It's always a lot easier to hit any target with a Winchester, or Greener, than the best handgun made.

A Smith and Wesson Schofield model is a deadly accurate weapon, in the hands of those who remain calm and deliberate. Hardy Tingwell proved to be neither. Dimwitted goober was a serious user of the spray-and-pray method. He simply put as much lead in the air as possible, and hoped to God he managed to hit something. His past efforts had most likely worked on locals, but not on us.

Concussion from the combined muzzle blasts of five or six blazing hand cannons set up a cloud of red dust that mingled with a heavy curtain of spent black powder. Gritty screen made the ability to see our attacker mighty tough, after about the first dozen or so shots. Figured we hadn't done much damage, because ole Hardy kept ripping off more rounds. Damned near everything he sent our way sounded like it hit Rip. My friend made too inviting a target.

Several seconds into the disagreement, I got the feeling someone I couldn't see might be involved in his efforts at our assassination. Bullets seemed to fly past my head from a number of different directions. When my hat flew off and dropped to the ground, about three feet to my right, I knew for certain at least one more shooter was behind us. Turned toward Rip, dug my toes in, and pushed him sideways.

We landed near the lip of the boardwalk. Four to six inches of overhanging lumber, and a rapidly rotting water trough, offered a small margin of shelter. The reddish-gray cloud bank had Hardy firing at a spot in the air, where he thought we still stood. I crawfished around so I could see back toward the Matador.

"You hit, Rip?" I yelled over my shoulder.

"Yeah. But don't think the poor shootin' dung weevil has done too much damage yet, Lucius."

Had barely got myself settled when a feller poked his

head from the alleyway between the hotel and Breedlove's store. Sent several well-placed shots his direction. Most splintered big chunks of wood from the building's framing as close to his bobbing noggin as I could get them. By then, I'd burned up all the powder in both pistols and had to go for the one in the holster snugged against my back. Set the back-shooting scum on his heels.

From the corner of my eye, I saw Boz hop from the jail's porch with a flame-spitting Colt in each hand. He walked directly toward the back-shooter's hidey-hole and fired a shot for every step he took. By the time he got to the middle of the street, the gunfire stopped as suddenly as it began. Got quiet enough for me to hear my wounded friend's ragged breathing.

Waited a second, or so, before I crawled over to help Rip. He'd rolled onto his back and held one saddlebag-sized paw over a spot in his upper chest; and at the same time, tried to cover a second hole in his lower right side with the other.

"How bad is it with you, friend?" I asked.

"Oh, had worse, Lucius. Gotta admit the one he put down low really pains me some. Hope it ain't so, but feels like the sorry skunk punched a hole in my gut."

Boz ran up, dropped to one knee beside his good friend, and said, "He ain't killed you, has he, Rip?"

"Don't think so, Boz, but he done went and hurt me—pretty good."

Boz jerked at the tail of Rip's bloody shirt. Ugly ragged hole, the size of my thumb, leaked life from a spot about two inches above the big man's gun belt. Boz ripped a chunk of the shirt away, wadded the faded material up, and stuffed it into the hole.

"Go get Doc Adamson, Lucius, and for Christ's sake hurry." The concern in Boz's voice shocked me into action.

12

"BASTARDS DO GET LUCKY"

THE ENTIRE HARDY Tingwell-led dustup took place but a few doors down from the doctor's office. Sawbones appeared through the drifting haze like an angel sent down from heaven about the time I'd taken my second step. Damn near ran into him.

People poured from the doorways of every shop and saloon to gawk. We moved Rip from the street to a leather-covered table in Adamson's office. Sawbones wouldn't let me, or Boz, stay while he tended our wounded amigo. Agitated physician forced us outside. Our strenuous objections at being excluded carried no weight. The doc proved right forceful when confronted with an emergency situation.

We found a place to sit on the boardwalk a few doors down the street. Boz said, "You see who did this, Lucius?"

"Hell, yes. Leastways, I saw one of them well enough to identify him. It was Hardy Tingwell. Crazier of the Tingwell bunch confronted us where Rip fell. Cussed us, drew first, and fired the opening volley. Happened damned quick. Got mighty hot before you stepped in and put a stop to it. Think if you hadn't got to the shooter behind us, we might've been looking up from the bottom of a newly dug grave tomorrow morning."

About then Ruby ran up, threw herself down beside me, and wept like a baby. She clung to my neck and kept saying, "God, I thought they'd killed you. I thought they'd killed you."

Took some serious talking before I finally got the girl calmed down enough to walk her back to the jail. Once we got inside, I thought she'd never stop kissing me. Course I didn't object much.

"Boz told me not to go outside, but I couldn't stay back here and not know what happened to you, Lucius."

"I know, darlin', but you needn't worry. Don't think any of these local badmen could hit a bull in the ass with a Napoleon cannon."

She rested her head on my chest and said, "Yes, but bastards do get lucky. Like the one who shot Rip. You know the old saying. Sometimes even a blind pig will find an acorn."

"Yeah, well, Hardy Tingwell is about as near being a blind pig as anyone walking upright can get when it comes to handling a pistol. Soon as I can locate his sorry self, I'm gonna see to it he spends the next few years in the state penitentiary for attempted murder of a Texas Ranger. Either that, or kill him deader than a fence post."

Ruby didn't like it one little bit when I made her stay inside. She said, "Morgan's dead. I don't have anything to fear now. No reason for me to hide any longer."

"Don't be too sure of that, darlin'," I countered. "His father and brother want revenge. They pointed the open muzzle of it at Rip and me today. Next time, they might come for you. Whole family's nuttier than your grandma's fruitcake. Just can't predict what they might try next. Woman-killing don't seem too far out of question for folks as loopy as these."

She did eventually calm herself enough for me to run back down the street and check on Rip. Doc said, "Man's got the constitution of a longhorn steer. Bullet hole up high wasn't as bad as it first appeared. Didn't hit anything of any great importance. Bounced off one of those conchos on his vest. Nick in his lower left side went all the way through. Have it plugged up now. If the bleeding stops, he'll be fine. Should the wound fester, he could yet die from blood poisoning. Pray for the first one, boys."

Boz stayed with Rip. He said, "You'd best keep a close eye on Ruby, Lucius. I'd be willing to bet my father's ranch Bull will kill the girl the first chance he gets." His dark assertion sounded mighty ominous to me. Took his advice. Stuck close to the jail for the next few days.

Turned out Rip had more hard bark clinging to his big ole self than we had any right to expect. He started getting better by the following morning. In spite of some blood loss, a right scary prognosis from Adamson, and the ever-present possibility of lethal infection, he sat up and demanded something to eat late that afternoon.

Two days after being shot, he'd pulled himself from the bed, and claimed he was more than ready to ride out and bring Hardy Tingwell to book for his crimes. Took Boz, me, the doc, and Ruby to get him back into bed with the promise that he'd do as told until his life was no longer in jeopardy.

Once the dust settled some, Boz and me talked about going out to the Tingwell place and dragging Hardy back by the scruff of the neck ourselves, or just shooting the hell out of him. Being as how there were only the two of us left, we had to discard any plans like that. Boz sent word to

Captain Culpepper as to our predicament. We asked for some reinforcements, but true to form, the captain simply wired back and informed us of the reality we faced.

Boz held the telegram out to arm's length and read, "Am unable to send you boys any assistance at this time. Have similar situations just as pressing in several other equally dangerous areas. Should the state of affairs deteriorate further, wire me immediately. Militia may be your only salvation. Remain certain you will find a way to bring about a suitable resolution to the problem. Good luck. Signed, Captain H. W. Culpepper."

"Damn, Boz. We're kind of hanging out in the breeze with our drawers down around our knees, aren't we?"

My friend dropped the message on Marshal Stonehill's desk. He sat for some time in deep thought and stared at the paper. Pushed it around with the tip of his finger as though he'd found a new form of bug that, while interesting, tended toward a state of creepy-crawly ugliness he didn't care for.

"You're right, Lucius, appears like we're totally alone and way out on a limb here. Awful part of the whole ugly shebang is that no matter how this mess turns out, we'll end up gettin' blamed if it goes bad."

We decided it best to stick close to town and hope the situation didn't get any worse. Two or three days passed and everything stayed pretty quiet. Course, such serenity tends toward lulling a man into a false sense of security.

Rip kept getting better. Ruby and I kept getting closer. Boz kept getting more nervous with each passing minute. Then, late on the afternoon of the third day, just about dusk, I found out why.

We'd settled into a pair of cane-bottomed chairs out on the boardwalk for what we hoped would be a peaceful evening of cigar smoke and manly bullshit. I'd almost snoozed off when I heard Boz mutter, "I'll just be damned to a smoldering, maggot-infested Hades. What new form of hell-sent devil have we got visiting with us now?"

Pushed my hat to the back of my head and glanced to the end of the street where he stared. Man on a pinto pony that looked tired enough to drop in its tracks came swaying into town. Feller wore a flat-brimmed black hat pulled low on his brow, faded-blue cotton shirt, large blood-red bandanna, and black canvas pants. Pair of silver-plated, bone-handled Colt pistols hung from a double-row cartridge belt that held a line of shotgun shells and a second row of .45-caliber pistol ammunition. Heavy, gold-inlaid English Greener rested across his saddle. Mahogany stock of the weapon appeared to have been polished to a high shine. An unlit cigar dangled from beneath his long droopy mustache. Red dust fogged up around him like he'd ridden straight from the gates of Hell.

Boz moaned, leaned forward, and rested his head in his hands. "Jesus Christ Almighty have mercy. As my grandfather always liked to say, just when you think it can't get any worse, it sure as hell does."

"You know him, Boz?"

"Yes, indeed. Think every lawman in Texas knows who he is, even if they've never had the pleasure of meeting the man face-to-face. His name's Ignatius Claude Winters. Few friends he ever had, who still count themselves among the living, call him Icy."

"You're just foolin' with me, right? Icy Winters? For real and true? Shotgun Winters? Highest-paid assassin living? Hear tell his name gets mentioned with almost every well-known murder for hire in the West."

"In the flesh. He could well be the meanest, most dangerous son of a bitch in Texas, Lucius. Personally, can't call to mind any man as bad. He's a perambulating dealer of death and destruction. Gonna be interesting to see which

way he jumps—Tingwell or Pitt. We should be able to sur-
mise something useful by the saloon he picks to tie up in
front of."

"Quincey Tull, a friend from over Waco way, said Winters comes into a town, visits the saloons, pool halls, and
barbershops, announces his presence, and offers to kill
anyone you'd like to have dead for three hundred dollars. Is
that true, Boz?"

"I've heard the same tale for years myself. It's true
enough that bodies usually start poppin' up in ditches
within a week or so after Icy's arrival—most of 'em shot-
gunned from behind. Be willing to bet my horse we'll have
dead Tingwell or Pitt riders turn up in a matter of days,
maybe even hours."

"We've got a full plate of problems without a skunk like
him making more."

"True enough. You know, I once spoke with a reputable
gent from over in Uvalde who claimed to have been getting
a shave the morning Icy made one of his offers. But as far
as I know, nobody has ever been able to prove such accusa-
tions. Good many folk with murdered relatives have tried.
Think he spends about as much time in court as most
crooked lawyers and easy-to-buy-off judges."

"Isn't he the one folks over in Comanche were absolutely certain murdered their sheriff?" I asked.

"Well, that's what they thought. And your rendition is
the tale what gets told anytime that particular killing is
mentioned. But thinkin' and provin' are about as far apart
as where we are from a full moon. Unfortunately, as was
the case with all the other murders attached to his name,
nobody in Comanche seen nothin'. He's one hell of a hard
killer to pin down."

We watched with newly focused interest as Winters

guided his stringy mustang to the front of the Matador, climbed down, and swaggered inside. Arrogant assassin rode right by us on his way to the saloon. Passed within thirty feet of our spot on the boardwalk. Never so much as acknowledged he'd seen us.

"Well, Boz, he picked the Tingwell crew's cow-country cantina. What do you think it means? Is he here to work for Bull, or to kill anyone who rides for the old man and has guts enough to show up at the Matador today?"

My friend slapped a dusty leg with his hat and said, "Don't know. Could be either one, I suppose."

"Thought you said we would be able to tell something from the saloon he picked."

"I've been wrong before, amigo."

"Not a very comforting assessment, ole son, given our situation. I mean, look at who's riding for Tingwell. John Roman Hatch, Casper Longstreet, and today, Icy Winters shows up and heads into the Matador. Our situation, as Cap'n Culpepper called it, seems to have got a lot worse in the passage of about two minutes."

Boz lowered his head, shook all over like a wet dog, and said, "Suppose we're gonna have to stroll over and talk with the murderous skunk for a spell."

"It's hotter'n hell under an iron skillet today, Boz. We go over there, interrupt the man's drinking, and we just might get him stirred up enough to start swapping lead. You sure you really want to brace him?"

"No, but we ain't got much choice in the matter, do we, amigo?"

"Guess not."

He grinned, stood, adjusted his weapons to a comfortable position, and hopped off the porch. "Come on, Lucius. Bring that short-barreled blaster, the ten-gauge. We've been sitting in the shade long enough. Might as well go pick a fight and, if ole Icy gets bulled up and the wax pops out of his ears, I want you to be able to splatter him all over at least three walls of the Matador."

13

"Murder Ain't Much of a Living"

GOT A SHADE over halfway across the dusty street when Boz stopped and said, "This time we'll play it a bit different. Kinda like that bank in Lone Pine. I'll wait by the front door, while you make your way to the back. Most likely, Winters picked the same table where we found Casper Longstreet sitting—the one in the far corner."

"Do we want to keep him seated?"

"Yeah. Make it harder for him to do much of anything. Door back there opens up on his left. Once I'm inside, you should detect the sound of me stomping around and such. You come in as soon as you hear me get close to the table. Couple of Rangers bracin' ole Icy ought to catch his undivided attention."

Played out exactly the way Boz wanted. Heard him clomp his way to Winters's corner. I pushed the door open, and stepped inside. Pulled it closed as quick as I could to let my eyes adjust to the low light. When our newest man-killer came into focus, his shifty-eyed stare raced back and forth from Boz to me.

Well-known eradicator of men seemed calm as a dipper of creek water when he said, "Do something for you fellers?"

Boz smiled. I followed his hard gaze back to the gun-man. Couldn't believe the silly mistake Winters had made. His custom-built weapon of choice stood in the corner, just about a fingertip's worth out of reach. I immediately felt a lot better about the whole situation. Figured if he made the slightest move toward the big popper, I could cut him apart like a stick of cheap baloney before he got halfway there.

Boz said, "Just wanted to chew the fat a spell, Icy."

Killer cut his eyes toward the shotgun again. "You know who I am, lawdog?"

"Your bloody reputation precedes you, Mr. Winters," I said.

"Ain't doin' nothin' wrong, Rangers. Just stopped in for a little somethin' to cut the dust. Rode hard to get here. My employer wanted me in town as quick as I could make it."

Boz stiffened. "And who might your employer be?"

"Local gent name of Tingwell sent word for me to burn leather getting here. Also provided me with a sizable re-tainer. Requested the performance of my *unique* services, should they be needed."

"Sent a sizable retainer for your 'unique services,' did he?" Boz spit what he said onto the table like a man con-fronted by something so disgusting it almost made him ill.

Winters flashed an emotionless grin and said, "Man's gotta make a living, Ranger."

Boz placed a booted foot in the chair facing Winters, leaned over on his raised knee, and sounded almost con-spiratorial when he said, "Murder ain't much of a living, Icy. We've had more'n our share of it here in Iron Bluff over the past few weeks. Upwards of half-a-dozen men done been caught short, and are deader'n hell in a Baptist preacher's backyard."

"Ain't nothing to me. I just rode into town."

"We've got pistol fighters and killers roaming the streets shooting folks down at will, and someone lynched a couple of cowboys a few miles outside town. Now you've shown up. Man of your exalted reputation tends to get our undivided attention. Makes hardworking lawmen like us wonder what might happen next."

"Ain't never kilt no one what didn't deserve to get dead, Ranger. I didn't come looking for no trouble. But be well aware that should it seek me out, I'll do whatever is necessary to make sure I'm not the one left in the street starin' at the sky from a pair of unblinking eyes."

Thought I'd see just how far I could push the man, so I said, "Hell, Boz, let's kill him now. Save ourselves all the trouble of having to do it later."

I'm certain my startling declaration surprised Boz, but I had my gaze fixed on Winters. Man's eyes flicked back and forth between the two of us real fast. Then his nerved-up glance darted toward the big Greener again. Figured he was trying to gauge how many times we could hit him before he managed to return fire. Right certain he came to the conclusion we'd turn him into a sieve if he moved.

Murdering snake leaned forward and placed his open palms on the table. Said, "I'll say it again. Ain't lookin' for no trouble. As you can see, ain't even properly armed. You boys appear to be upright, God-fearin' types to me. Have serious doubts you'd shoot an innocent man th'out givin' him a chance."

A low chuckle clawed its way to Boz's throat. "Don't bet your life on it, Winters. My partner here, Lucius "By God" Dodge, would just soon kill you as spit—if I tell him he can. Besides, the only innocent period of your life was sometime before your fourteenth birthday. Seems I recall that year being about the time you killed your first man, over in Uvalde. Used a nine-inch butcher's knife on him, if memory serves. Carved him up like a Christmas turkey."

Our newest badman in town got to squirming around in his chair like someone had lit a fire on the floor under his seat. Saw his lip quiver when he said, "Wait a minute now. Let's don't get too hasty here. I'm just a man tryin' to get by. Sell my services to make enough money so I can eat. No need for you boys to take a testy stance with me yet. Maybe someday down the road, but not right now."

Boz turned to me again. "Could be he's right, Lucius. Reckon we'll let Mr. Winters go his way." He motioned me to the door. We backed out through the saloon's batwings. As we hit the boardwalk, turned, and headed for the jail, Boz said, "Mighty nervy move you made back there, Lucius. Damn near scared me slap to death. But you know, I think we just mighta put a smidgen of the fear of God in Mr. Icy Winters. And when it comes right down to the nut-cutting, every little bit helps."

We strolled over to Doc Adamson's office and told Rip all about our most recent version of boot-wearing shotgun-toting hell. He reacted about the same way Boz had.

"Wouldn't have no trouble killin' him outright myself," he said. Course his suggestion sounded like a fine idea to me.

Later that evening, Boz and I watched Winters mosey out of town. Little doubt he was headed for Tingwell's ranch. Boz said, "Be willing to bet an iron nickel against a Tennessee walking horse, ole Bull will have his crew back in town raisin' hell soon as he and Icy have come to an agreement on price."

"Would be something of a relief if a few of the hired gunfighters on either side got their comeuppance, don't you think? So far only people who've managed to get dead have been run-of-the-mill cowboys who couldn't hit a seventeen-hand hay-burner from ten feet away."

"You mean with the exception of Morgan Tingwell, don't you, Lucius?"

"Yeah. Keep forgetting about him."

"Think it best you keep his cold corpse somewhere near the front part of your memory. Personally, I don't believe we've heard the last of his unfortunate departure for hell's front gate."

We ragged around on the thing and worried over it some more, but a week went by—and nothing happened. Got so quiet around town at night you could smell the odor of uneasy silence. Boz allowed as how the number of honest-to-God man-killers on either side of the problem might have brought things to a much-desired standoff. Amazing how a feller's mind can lull him into such foolish thinking.

We'd stopped to chew the fat with Horace Breedlove; one hotter'n green-eyed hell morning, when a bunch of kids who'd been down on the river fishing ran up. They were all barefoot, dragged cane poles, and talked a mile a minute. Took us a spell to calm them down. Boz finally had to pull one out of the group and just talk with him.

"Now what's the problem, son?"

Boy could barely catch his breath. Appeared he and the others had run all the way from the Angelina. "We wuz a-fishing in ole man Bronson's stock tank, just off the river, 'bout three miles out of town toward Mr. Pitt's ranch. Caught a nice little mess of sunfish on worms and wuz on our way back home. Ran upon this dead feller in the ditch."

"Where'd you see him?" I asked.

Towheaded boy snatched a chewed-up straw hat from his near-white-haired noggin, scratched, and said, "Oh, near three miles out on the west side of the road, Ranger.

We'd walked up the east side going. Didn't see him then. Can't miss him comin' back, though. He's a-layin' on his back a-starin' at the sky like he expected to spot angels comin' down from heaven or somethin'."

"Have you ever seen him before?" Boz asked.

Boy puzzled over the question long enough to slap the hat back on his head and said, "Think so. He mighta been one of Mr. Pitt's riders. Seems like I seen him a-comin' outta the Fin and Feather, wunst or twicest. Some of them other cowboys mighta called him Arlo. Yeah, that's his name, Arlo."

Boz and I saddled up. Headed out as fast as we could. I told Ruby to stay inside till we got back. Kids pinpointed the dead man's location within a few steps. He fell exactly the way they'd described. No observable wounds on the body till Boz rolled him over. Bunched-up gob of lead from a scattergun had punched a hole in his back the size of my fist. All that shot damned near blew the shirt and vest he wore to ribbons.

Boz knelt beside the body, wiped sweat from his dripping brow, and said, "Jesus. Winters must've been right on top of the boy when he blasted hell out of him. This poor brush-popper never knew what hit him."

"Are we sure Winters did the killing?" I asked.

Boz shrugged. "Who else could have, or would have, for that matter? Hell, we talked about his methods the other day when he came into town. Arlo's murder fits right into the stories I've heard for years. Icy hits town, men start dying right and left. Bet this murder is just the beginning."

"You think Romulus Pitt will stand still for the continued bushwhacking of his men like this?"

"Not damned likely. Soon as he finds out that another of his boys has been murdered, he'll have Fox and Clements out looking for bloody revenge. Feud's been a hot'n so far,

Lucius, but I'm afraid this war's about to get a lot hotter."

We gathered up the dead cow-chaser's still-leaking corpse. Loaded him across the saddle of my horse. I rode back to town behind Boz. Had barely passed the jail when we noticed a lot of fevered activity around Doc Adamson's office.

Boz said, "Hell's bells, that ain't a good sign by a damned sight."

Hermione Blackstock ran up. Between the running and the crying, poor woman had trouble catching her breath. Took a spell before we were able to make out something like, "He shot her. Right in front of my café."

"What are you trying to say, Hermione?" I asked. "Who got shot?"

Took another second or so before she barely breathed, "Ruby. She came over from the jail and asked me to fix her something light for lunch. Bull Tingwell came storming up." Hermione clutched her throat. "Shot her while we stood on the boardwalk talking. Crazy old coot yelled, 'That's for killing my son, you hell-spawned bitch.' She fell right at my feet. Doc's got her over in his office. It looks bad, Lucius, real bad."

Dropped my reins into Boz's outstretched hand and heeled it down the street. Hit Doc Adamson's door like a battering ram. He made a grab for me as I stumbled toward Ruby's limp body. Sweet God Almighty! Appeared to me as though her life had sprayed onto everything the eye could behold. Rip helped Doc shove me back to the boardwalk.

Adamson leaned against my chest with both hands and said, "You've got to stay out here, Lucius. She's been badly hurt, and if I can't stop the bleeding—she's going to die. Do you understand me, son?" Man's words fell on my heart like an anvil dropped from heaven.

Rip tried to reassure me when he added, "He's doin' what he can, Lucius. You can't help. Let the man get back to savin' her."

Over the years, I've come to the firm belief there's just nothing to match the agony of waiting to find out if someone you love will live or die. I'd met Ruby under the strangest of circumstances. Fallen for her in an equally outlandish way, instigated by the girl herself. In truth, we barely knew each other. None of that mattered. My feelings for her were just as intense as those of any man who'd known the woman he loved for a lifetime. Now, those feelings had been turned against me by the insane act of a man determined to bring about the death, or destruction, of anyone other than his own family.

Boz and I sat in chairs outside Doc's office. Boz said, "She'll be fine, Lucius. I have complete confidence in Adamson's ability. Besides, you two were meant for each other. I could tell it the first time I saw her look at you."

"You've no idea how true that statement is, Boz."

"What do you mean, I've no idea?"

Turned, and tried to nail him to his seat with a hard-eyed stare. "You must promise not to tell Ruby what I'm about to say. Got to promise, Boz, or I can't let out a word about something I've never told anyone see the light of day."

A strange look settled on his craggy face as he rubbed the stubble on his chin. "Okay. I promise. Won't tell anyone, especially Ruby."

"Well, some years ago an old woman people called Witch Hazel lived in a shack out on a bayou off the North Fork of the Bosque River, about ten miles from Waco."

Never knew Boz Tatum had a fear of haints and such, but he said, "Sweet Jesus, witches scare the hell out of me, Lucius. You had nothin' to do with her, did you, son?" Then he performed some strange hand signs as if to ward off evil spirits.

"Kinda. Me and a friend went out sneaking around her house one night. Old lady caught me. Grabbed my ear and almost twisted it off. Dragged me into her house. Thought for sure she was going to cook me up like a jackrabbit in her stew pot."

"Oh, God, I would have died right on the spot. Done been buried for more years than I've been alive if a witch got hold of me." More hand signs. Then he went to spitting in every direction of the compass. His eyes rolled into the back of his head. For a second I thought he'd had some kind of fit, or maybe a stroke, but he finally came back.

"Well, she sat me down in front of this big stone fireplace. Said, 'Don't you move now, boy, lest I says you can. You hear.' Damn near scared the bejabbers out of me."

"Done went and put a hex on you, didn't she, Lucius? Paralyzed your dumb little ass with an unspoken curse."

"No. She merely scared the strength out of my spindly legs. Anyway, she pulled a Bible up off the floor. Biggest Bible I ever saw. Monstrous thing bound in tooled leather with a wooden cross attached to the front. She sat it on a squatty piece of table between us and said, 'Open the Book, boy.'"

Honestly, I thought Boz would pass out right in front of me. "Oh, no. Here comes the bad news. I just know it."

"Not quite. She pointed at the Bible and said, 'Run your finger along the page and stop anywhere you feel the urge, but don't look.'"

"Did you do it?"

"Of course I did."

"Then what?"

"I stopped, and she said, 'Read from where your finger

landed.' So I read it. Never forgot what it said. Short passage was from Revelations. 'I will give him the morning star.' Ole Witch Hazel stiffened up like a petrified fence post. Almost fell out of her chair, right onto the floor."

"That it? She let you go then?"

"No. Crazed woman grabbed my hand, turned it over, and started tracing the lines with the broken nail of a knotted finger. Staked me to the chair with a pair of the bluest eyes I've ever seen and said, 'One day you'll meet a beautiful, red-haired angel. She will come to you during a most queer and deadly time. You must cleave to her. *She* is the morning star. But never forget, stars disappear when the sun comes up. Now, git, before I'm forced to skin you alive and stretch your hide over my windows to keep out the bad weather.' "

"Witches' curses. Witches' curses. Always made it a point to stay away from them kind of batty women. My ole granny told me long ago that such folk were in league with Satan himself. Ain't had no lingering bad effects from your visit, have you, Lucius?" A strange look came over him as he stared at me. For a second, I felt as though I'd grown another head during our conversation.

"Well, there is one thing. Sometimes, late at night, I can still hear that old woman's cackling laughter in my brain as I ran from her ramshackle cabin."

More outlandish hand signs and spitting. "Sweet Merciful Father, Lucius."

"Nothing to it until now, Boz. In fact, I'd not so much as given the event a second's worth of consideration until recently. All of a sudden the predictions of that strange and eventful night, so long ago, have come back to the forefront of my thoughts. No doubt about it, Witch Hazel was right, Boz. Ruby is the morning star. Exactly the way she promised the girl to me."

Boz muttered something that sounded like, "Harrumph,

harrumph, harrumph," then lapsed into silence. Got the impression he didn't want to talk about witches, or other such phantasms, any further. Guess if the circumstances had played out even the slightest bit different, it would have been humorous. Longer I thought on his odd behavior, the more potential for funning with him emerged, but I decided to let it pass until another time.

We waited. Took Doc Adamson near three hours of serious doctor work before he came out and told us we could come inside and see Ruby.

Boz said, "You go ahead, Lucius. Don't imagine the girl needs two of us yammerin' at her at the same time. Talk with her, if you can. I'll wait here."

Doc pulled at my sleeve as I turned toward the door. He said, "From what I've heard, witnesses saw Bull Tingwell fire at least four times before he put the spur to his animal. He hit Ruby twice. She must have been turned kind of sideways. One bullet grazed the back of her head. Didn't do much damage, but the crease it left bled plenty—typical of scalp wounds."

"And the other?"

Adamson rubbed his brow with a shaking hand. I noticed black blood caked under his fingernails. He said, "The second punched through the fleshy part of her upper left arm, nicked a rib, and lodged inside her chest. I had a tough time locating it. Hadn't been for going through her arm, the slug would probably have killed her outright. Took me some serious knife work to get that bullet out. No doubt about it, mighty touchy situation, Lucius. Recovery could take months—maybe more. No way to foretell the outcome. Just have to pray for the best. She's weak from loss of so much blood, so don't stay long."

The hours of waiting had been somewhere just this side of awful. But when I saw Ruby laid out, her pale face drained of so much life, a fury grew inside me the likes of which I'd never known. She didn't move when I touched her hand, and failed to respond to my most tender kiss.

I sat with her all night. Next morning, she woke briefly. Just long enough to whisper, "I'm so tired," and drift back to the blackness of sleep. Thought she recognized me, but couldn't tell for certain.

Hermione came in after the breakfast rush. Spelled me so I could get down to the jail for a bit of food and a nap. Boz and Rip sopped biscuits in milk gravy and barely cooked eggs when I pushed the door open. Both men stood, offered their regrets and concerns about what had happened. We ate in silence, until the door popped open and Bronson Stonehill stepped inside.

Boz said, "Well, well, well. And to what do we owe the honor of an appearance by Iron Bluff's absentee marshal?"

Stonehill removed his hat, and toed at the rough plank floor like a chastised kid. "Done got word as how Bull Tingwell went and shot a woman. Any man who'd stoop that low needs to swing, as far as I'm concerned."

Rip dropped his fork, took a healthy swig of black coffee, swallowed, then said, "It's true enough. Bastard put two slugs in Miss Ruby Black. You can blubber around about concern all you want, but the question that needs an answer has to be, what's it to you?"

Stonehill's face reddened. Fingers of his hand scratched at a spot above the grips of a well-oiled Colt's pistol. "Well, by God, I'm still the marshal hereabouts. Ain't nobody gonna shoot women in my town and get away with it as long as I'm still breathing."

I said, "Seems I recall you telling me and Boz, right after we arrived, that you were Romulus Pitt's man. Ain't that true?"

That made him even madder. "Don't mean a damned

thing. If Pitt had done an equally gutless deed, I'd harbor nothing less than the same kind of anger."

Boz shook his head. "Made you mad, huh? What the hell do you figure on doin' about it?"

Stonehill shot back, "Snatch the woman-shootin' son of a bitch up, throw him in jail, wait to see if Miss Ruby recovers, and put him on trial for whatever we can. If she dies, we build a gallows in the town square and hang him."

Boz snickered and snorted, "Well, by God, sounds easier'n gettin' stuck in East Texas mud."

Stonehill shook his head like a man who'd grown weary of the conversation. "Catchin' Tingwell is a lot easier than you know, Ranger Tatum."

Man got my attention. "How's that?" I asked.

Iron Bluff 's marshal smiled. "Because I know where he is every afternoon about four o'clock."

His revelation got my attention. I said, "And where would that be, Marshal?"

All of a sudden Stonehill had a captive audience, and liked the feel of it. "The Tingwells had several daughters when they arrived. One of 'em was a beautiful child. She didn't look, or act, like any of the rest of that bunch. Everyone around town commented as how that blond-haired beauty was gifted with the face of an angel. Unfortunately, she died of the putrid throat about six months after the Tingwells arrived."

Think we all mumbled "Diphtheria" at the same time. Tragedy of such a prospect even had the power to elicit sympathy for scum like Tingwell. Nothing more heartrending than the knowledge of a child passing to the Maker from the effects of a grisly disease.

Stonehill said, "Yeah. Name was Julia. She had three sisters. Every one of them uglier'n a mud fence and meaner'n hell-on-a-stick."

"What does the child's death have to do with where Tingwell is every day?" I asked.

Marshal swelled up with the pride derived from secret knowledge and said, "Well, between four and five this afternoon, I'd bet everything I own you can find him visiting the little girl's grave. Family buried her on a hill atop a bluff overlooking the Angelina. Most important of all, he's always insisted on making the visit alone."

Boz scratched his chin. "Now that *is* some valuable information."

Rip got an agitated look on his face and said, "Yeah, but hell, boys, that'd be pretty damned low, wouldn't it? Go out and snatch a man away from his grief at the grave of his dead daughter. Sweet Jesus! Sounds downright awful to me."

Got my dander up. "Damnit it, Rip, I'd go right to Hell's doorstep and fight the devil himself to bring that old bastard in for what he did to Ruby. Just no excusing that or any of the other killings he's most likely responsible for since we arrived in town. I say we burn leather to the grave, jerk him up short, and drag his sorry ass back here."

Boz stared directly into my eyes when he said, "Hardy ain't gonna like us takin' his father one bit. Bet the murderous snake will be outside our door in a heartbeat, with blood in his eyes and smoke pourin' out of his pistols, 'fore we can get our breath back from the ride."

I said, "Don't give a bucket of cold spit what that pea-brained idiot likes or don't like. Time has come for the Tingwell bunch to pay for some of their crimes against this community—up to and including what Bull did to Ruby." I tried not to leave Boz much room to crawfish on the question.

He stood, rearranged all his belts and weapons. Cinched his hat down tight, turned to Stonehill, and said, "Lead the way, Marshal."

Rip jumped out of his chair, grimaced a bit when he stretched some of his stitches, and shouted, "Damned right. Let's fetch him back and lock him in the cell farthest from the door."

Boz placed a hand on his friend's shoulder and said, "Stonehill can show me and Lucius where to find him, Rip. You're still in no real shape to be ridin', and you know it." Thorn started to protest, but gave up with a sigh of resignation and flopped back into his chair.

Ten minutes later me, Boz, and Stonehill were kicking hard for a spot on the Angelina. I came to the sobering realization, after we got out of town, that our questionable guide could well be leading us into a trap. But I didn't care. Righteous truth of the matter flared up and slapped any arguments against the raid to the back of an agitated mind. Only thing I could think about involved the pleasure of seeing the look on Bull Tingwell's face when I threw his sorry woman-shooting ass in a jail cell and turned the key. Could hear the lock snap into place over the pounding of our horse's thundering hooves.

14

"I'll Hang You and Romulus Myself"

STONEHILL LED US off the road about midway between Iron Bluff and Tingwell's ranch. We followed him down a wide trail through heavy stands of cedar and pine that quickly turned to cottonwood and blackjack oak the closer we got to the river. About a mile into the trees, we started on a steady, but easy, climb that kept moving upward for most of a half hour.

The heavy growth of trees eventually petered out. Our guide reined us up at the edge of a grassy field and pointed to the hill's crest. At the peak a splendid oak, shaped in the image of a giant mushroom, spread enormous limbs over an open area of shaded cool for any visitor willing to stop and visit. Through binoculars, we could see the old man seated on a piece of granite that rested at the head of an iron fence.

Stonehill said, "Bull had that chunk of rock shipped here all the way from somewhere in Arkansas."

"Arkansas?" Boz mumbled.

"Yep. Folks up there, around Petit Jean Mountain, chiseled it out in the shape of a chair. He had it placed at the head of Julia's grave, then built that fence around the whole shebang. Comes up every afternoon and brings fresh-cut flowers."

"That's it? Just brings flowers?" I asked.

"No, flowers are simply the beginning. He sits in his cold hard chair and weeps like a baby for hours. Don't know 'bout you boys, but I ain't never seen anything to match it."

"Grief for a departed youngster can have strange effects on people," Boz said. "I've seen folks mourn themselves into a grave, right beside their dead children. Sad, really sad."

Pulled one of my pistols and checked the loads. Cocked it and said, "Well, I suppose if we stood here for another year or two, Bull just might grieve himself to death sitting on his granite throne. But he's got the attempted murder of Ruby Black to answer for, I figure. Along with a good many other crimes we don't now have witnesses for. Let's go gather him up. Drag his sorry self to jail."

Boz said, "You'll notice my young friend has turned into a hard case over the years, Marshal Stonehill. Not much for flowery words when it comes to criminals."

Stonehill nodded, then pointed to a faint footpath leading to Julia Tingwell's elaborate tomb. He said, "Bull won't see us till we're right on top of him if we go this way."

"Looks fine to me," Boz said as he breeched his shotgun, dropped shells into both chambers, and snapped it shut again. We'd been thinking along the same lines, because he added, "You go ahead, Marshal. Lucius and I'll follow. Be aware, if this has even a sniff of turning into an ambush, I can personally gar-un-damn-tee you'll be the first to die."

Stonehill didn't look surprised in the least when he said, "Don't harbor much faith in your fellowman, do you, Tatum?"

I said, "You misunderstand, Marshal. Boz and me have the greatest of trust in our fellowmen. But when it comes to those who've worked in the service of belligerents that have already made efforts to kill us, we tend to get a little jumpy in a pinch."

Stonehill threw a disgusted glance at each of us, grunted, then tied his animal to a scruffy bush and headed up the hill. We followed, and stayed as close on his heels as the trail allowed.

Bull couldn't have picked a more beautiful spot. Patches of yellow, red, purple, and blue wildflowers covered young Julia's final resting place, and appeared to flourish in spite of the blistering heat.

The footpath Stonehill led us up came out behind Tingwell's massive granite chair. We slipped up on him. The man never even moved. Boz whispered, "Hell, I think he's asleep."

An open Bible lay across the old bastard's lap, and he'd slumped to one side like a sleeping baby. Hell, his guiltless repose, at the grave of a dead daughter, was enough to bring tears to my sainted white-haired grandmother's ancient eyes, but not mine.

I crept up on his right side and, gently, lifted his pistol from its holster. He stirred, then snapped awake like a branded bobcat. As he bounded to unsteady feet and made a grab for his missing weapon, the Bible fell and landed against the iron fence surrounding the grave.

"What the hell's goin' on?" he yelled. "You badge-totin' skunks got no right to be here. This is consecrated ground, you sons of bitches. No one's allowed on my baby's sacred gravesite but me or members of my family."

Boz sounded almost regretful when he said, "Sorry to interrupt your spiritual contemplations of the Great Beyond, Mr. Tingwell. Under normal circumstances, I would never think of committing such an inconsiderate act. But you shot Ruby Black, right in front of Hermione Blackstock's café, and we're here to arrest you for that act of reckless violence."

Bull didn't bother to deny Boz's accusation. Sounded almost proud when he said, "Hell, I told that evil bitch I'd kill her first chance I got. Fair warning is fair warning, far as I'm concerned. She shoulda been carrying the rifle she kilt my son with. Least she'd of had a chance when I started shootin'."

Surprised the hell out of him when I said, "Well, you came close to murder, Mr. Tingwell. Unfortunately, your aim must have failed you. Kind of thing tends to happen when a man gets your age."

"What the hell do you mean by my aim failed me?"

"You didn't kill her, Bull. She's still alive. Gonna testify at your trial. Way things look right now, you'll soon have the pleasure of getting to know fellers like Cock-Eyed Bob Matoose real well when the law sends you down to Huntsville for about thirty years. Way I hear the story told, Bob likes to dance and needs a new partner."

Our defanged mountain lion shook with rage. "Just be damned if I'll ever see one day in prison. You lock me in a cell and I can promise you bastards my only living son, Hardy, along with Hatch, Longstreet, and Icy Winters, will kill all three of you before sunrise the next day."

Boz grabbed the old man by his collar, pulled him up to where their noses almost touched, and growled, "That could well happen. Knowing you for the woman-shooting skunk you are, we fully expect your whole murderous clan to be in town before nightfall. But I'm giving instructions to my partner, right here and right damned now, if any of us Rangers manages to get *accidentally,* or *deliberately,* shot, whichever of us is remaining should hang you immediately."

The old man's face went purple. "You wouldn't dare such a thing," he roared.

"Try me, Tingwell. I've suffered about as much of this fussin', feudin', and fightin' between your bunch and the Pitts as I'm willing to put up with. If necessary, I'll hang you and Romulus myself in order to bring the whole mess to a suitable ending."

Boz wasn't quite finished. He shoved Tingwell away and shook his finger in the man's face, then said, "Never think for a second I don't have the power, or the will, for such an act."

After a few seconds of silence, he brought the entire argument to an end when he turned to Stonehill and me. "Put this old goat on his horse. Let's get the hell out of here before some of his family comes lookin' for him."

Tingwell still didn't go easy. Fought us every step of the way. We scrapped around with him till I grew weary of it. 'Bout the time it looked like Boz might take his rifle barrel to the old man's head, me and Stonehill latched onto Bull and dragged him to his horse.

Eventually, we had to bind his hands. He still jumped off his horse twice, and fell off once. Tied him to his animal before we were finally able to get started on our way back to town. Boz mumbled something about throwing a loop over Tingwell's neck and dragging him back to town. Think he could well have done it, but for having me and Stonehill along.

Our small posse's arrival in Iron Bluff caused quite a stir. Swarm of locals gathered in front of the jail. Sun was on its way down, but the blistering heat had every member of the delegation mopping their sweaty brows. Dust and horseflies billowed around us as we reined up.

Dragged Bull off his horse, and hustled him into the jail quick as we could. Goodly bit of quarrelsome behavior erupted from the crowd when they recognized him. A few yelled curses at the man. Most stood silently and looked uneasy. Got the impression no real enthusiasm existed for what we'd done. Hell, I didn't care whether they liked it or not.

We'd barely slammed the cell door on our newest prisoner when a group of the town's leading citizens pushed their way into Stonehill's office. *Weekly Sentinel*'s editor led the delegation and did most of the talking.

Cloud Quigley said, "Ranger Tatum, think you know Horace Breedlove, Andy Nash, and these others. We've been talking it over, and would like to know your intentions concerning Mr. Tingwell."

Boz let a steady gaze sweep over the group as he said, "I intend to hold *Mr. Tingwell* until we can get Judge Stanley Cooper over from Shelbyville for a trial. If justice can be served, I personally have little doubt Bull will be found guilty of attempted murder, at the very least. Course that will depend on whether or not Ruby Black dies. I expect, if she manages to stay alive, he'll be sent to prison for a spell—most likely the rest of his wretched life. Should the girl pass on, I'll personally take no end of pleasure in seeing him hang."

A palpable sense of uneasiness swept over Iron Bluff's leading citizens. Quigley gritted his teeth. "You must understand, sir, we've talked this over and are very concerned about the actions you gentlemen have taken."

Banker Ezra Crowe stepped out of the assembly. He waved a shaking hand at the group of friends as if to include them in his comments. "While everyone here supports your feelings on this matter, we have a sense that you men might not recognize the threat your actions bring to our doorstep, Rangers. You know, as well as we do, that Tingwell employs the most lethal gang of gunmen in the state. They could well turn whatever ire his incarceration brings on us."

Their stunning pronouncements surprised the hell out of me. Never, for one minute, did I figure on such a response when we set out to bring our prisoner in for Ruby's shooting. I'm certain their words had the same effect on Boz and Rip. Not sure about Stonehill. He remained something of a mystery—a man to be carefully watched in spite of his recent change of heart. Extremely hard for me to believe, but the townsfolk of Iron Bluff appeared bent on backing away from whatever support they may have harbored for us upon our arrival.

Jerked every head my direction when I snapped, "I don't want to hear this load of cow-fritters."

Rip said, "Calm down, Lucius."

"Damned if I will. Bull Tingwell shot a woman outside the door of one of Iron Bluff's leading businesses. If you people think, for a second, we're gonna let this four-tailed skunk go, you'd best think two or three more times."

Boz said, "Lucius is right. Bull is staying in a nice comfortable cell until Judge Cooper can make it over from Shelbyville."

I respected Ezra Crowe. Safe to say I even liked the man—given what little I knew of him. But when he said, "Your actions could well get some of us killed, Ranger," I damn near puked my socks up.

Something inside me snapped like a rotten cottonwood limb. I took a step toward Iron Bluff's delegation of spineless wonders and snapped, "Get out of here—right now. I'll not suffer such foolishness. Tingwell stays. That's the end of it."

Boz stepped between me and Crowe. He placed a quieting hand on my shoulder, then turned to face the antsy group of Iron Bluff citizens. "Best take it on out of here, folks. Get my young friend here stirred up, and I can't be responsible for what might happen."

Whole spineless bunch hustled out. They all acted like their feet had caught fire. But, as it turned out, the self-appointed group's hasty departure didn't end our day of troubles and woe. Hell, no, not by a damned sight. Jail door had barely snapped shut when the rumble from a sizable number of horses passed in the street out front, and stopped next door at the Fin and Feather.

Stonehill snatched off his hat, then shook his head like a tired dog and said, "Pitt's crew. Bet he'll be paying you boys a visit shortly."

Words had barely passed his lips when we heard the older Pitt call from the street. "Got business with you Rangers. Step on out. Let's talk."

Boz glanced around the room. "Shotguns for everyone." Stonehill grabbed one down from his gun rack. Boz said, "You don't have to go out with us if you don't want to, Rip. Lucius and I can handle it."

Thorn acted insulted. "Damned if I'm gonna stay inside with all this stuff happenin'."

Checked the loads in my weapon and said, "You've got to stay with Tingwell, Rip. You're our last line of defense. Pitt and his gang of killers gets past us, you'll have to keep them away from the old man, or kill him. Personally, I'd go with killin' him."

Could tell Rip cared not a lick for my assessment, but he simply nodded his agreement, headed to the cell block, and locked the inner door behind him. Heard him tell Tingwell, "Don't worry, Bull. If any of Pitt's crew gets past the door, you'll be just fine—real dead, but fine."

Stonehill said, "I'll stand with you boys. Guess now's as good a time as any for Pitt to know I'm no longer with him. Besides, I've been ready for a return to my sworn duties as marshal of Iron Bluff for a long time now. Let's do it."

I pulled the door open, and the three of us gingerly moved onto the jail's rough-cut plank porch. Six barrels of buckshot leveled up on Pitt's pack of quarrelsome dogs. Romulus sat on his tall horse between Nick Fox and Alvin Clements. Eli and Pruitt held places behind their father, as though to guard his back. At least ten other riders surrounded the group's central core of leaders.

Entire front rank of the heavily armed group looked a bit surprised when Stonehill took the spot on Boz's left. Restless stir of uneasiness spread through the congregation like Beelzebub himself had shown up and staked out the front pew of a prayer meeting.

Romulus Pitt growled, "What the hell are you doin', Stonehill? Get your sorry ass over here."

"Not today, Mr. Pitt. Not from now on either. These men are right about what they've done, and why they're here. Gonna do my job the right way—for a change. Ain't gonna be no more favorin' anybody, or any group. Might as well make up your mind to it."

"I'll be damned. You're bought and paid for. So, I'll see you by my side, on a horse ridin' the hell out of town, or dead. You choose."

Everyone in attendance appeared stunned, including Pitt, the day Stonehill stood his ground. My admiration for the man went up several notches when he said, "Sorry, but you're wrong, Mr. Pitt. Good people of Iron Bluff put me in office by way of a legally held election. I'm bound by my oath of office, and good for at least another year."

The elder Pitt's face flushed. For about a second, I thought his head might explode. When he didn't respond to

Stonehill's startling revelation, Eli shook a finger our direction and yelped, "We came for Bull Tingwell. Don't give a hatful of horseshit what you're about, Marshal Stonehill." The word "marshal" came out like it was something soft and mushy he'd stepped in that smelled bad.

Romulus raised a hand to shush his blustering son and said, "Nobody's about to get away with shooting a woman in my town—least of all one of the damned Tingwells. We came here to see justice done. Might not be now. Might not be today. Might not even be next week. But by God, I will see justice done."

I could tell Boz was within spitting distance of losing his patience when he snapped, "Soon as Judge Stanley Cooper arrives, justice will be done. But it ain't gonna have nothing to do with you or these others you've brought with you." Men behind Pitt stirred again. Couldn't tell if their restlessness had its basis in a fear of what might happen or a desire for the dance to commence in earnest.

"We'll see about that," Pitt snarled.

"Yes, we will," Boz shot back. "Right now, it'd be in your best interest to take all these boys over to the Fin and Feather. 'Bout time for all of you to cool off and have a drink."

Thought I'd get right to the point and put the reality of the situation to them straight up, so they couldn't miss it. "You're looking down six barrels of instant death, Mr. Pitt. Get your people away, right now, or there's gonna be a bloodbath. Close as you are to me, I can promise you'll be the first to die."

Think I caught everyone by surprise. Front rank of Pitt's band of gunmen got to blinking real fast. Whole gang pulled their mounts one step back. Then they all focused on their leader for guidance. Pitt remained motionless. He looked to be boiling alive in a bottomless pit of oily hatred.

Pruitt, who appeared to have about a half a dipper more brains than his mouthy brother, urged his mount up beside Romulus, leaned sidways in his stirrups and whispered something in his father's ear. The older Pitt's hands moved away from his gun belt and went to the lapels of his vest.

After about a second or so of silence, Romulus said, "Hell, we can take care of this anytime, boys. Judge Cooper won't be here for weeks. Lots can happen in two or three weeks. Come on. I'll buy all of you a round of drinks." As the group turned their animals and ambled toward Pitt's saloon, he added, "Damned fortunate for you lawdogs I'm in a good mood; otherwise you'd all be dead, and Bull Tingwell's sorry old ass would be swinging from that tree yonder."

I started to tell the insolent bastard how the cow ate the cabbage, but Boz whispered, "Let it go, Lucius. The storm's blowin' over. Ain't no need for us to piss him off any further today if we can help it."

Course he was right. Watched until all Pitt's boys had vacated the street and disappeared into the Fin and Feather. We were on the verge of breathing a well-needed sighs of relief when I heard Stonehill say, "Oh, shit. What now?"

Hardy Tingwell thundered up in front of us at the head of his personal collection of man-killers and pistoleers. Every damned one of them looked totally pissed and ready for a fight.

15

"The Son of a Bitch Is Bluffin'"

BOZ MUMBLED, "PITT'S visit was something of a surprise. I actually expected to see these boys first."

Thick cloud of red dust swirled around Hardy Tingwell, and all those out front, as their horses danced to a nervous, tail-twitching stop. Hardy stood in his stirrups and said, "Came for my father, boys. Either give him up or we'll tear this jail down and take him."

Boz brought his big boomer to bear on the boy, and snugged the stock into his shoulder. Stonehill and I followed his lead.

"Make a move that brings you one more foot my direction, and I'll blast you right into Satan's front parlor," Boz snapped.

John Roman Hatch separated himself from the crowd, and eased up beside the only living Tingwell son left. As if by magic, the skeletal Casper Longstreet appeared next to Hatch.

"Where's Winters?" I realized real quick that Boz's question was directed at me as much as Hatch, Hardy, or any of the others.

Identical, smirky grins spread across the Tingwell gang's faces. Hatch said, "He's feeling a bit sickly today. Been working right hard the past week or so. You know how it is, Rangers. Poor boy's just wore down to a nubbin a-practizin' his chosen trade."

Snickering, overconfident laughter started in the front rank and spread to the rear. Boz shocked hell out of me and Stonehill when he jumped off the plank porch, marched over to Hatch, and shoved the shotgun muzzle right into the gunman's oversized silver belt buckle. Too late, many of the Tingwell bunch realized they'd committed the unforgivable sin. Never laugh at a man like Boz Tatum. Such an act could get you delivered into a pine box in a heartbeat.

Honest to God, felt like the world stopped spinning. Street got quieter than the inside of a freshwater clam. Everyone there heard Boz when he snarled, "I've had one hell of a bad day, Hatch. Woke up with a dull headache that's been rackin' my noggin ever since me and Lucius arrived in this stinky armpit of a town. Just had to do this same dance with Romulus Pitt. I'm gettin' tired of the lot of you real damned quick." He pulled the shotgun back about an inch, and then shoved it deeper into the flesh of Hatch's belly.

John Roman's face contorted in pain. "Careful, Tatum. Sure wouldn't want that thing to go off by accident."

Hardy snorted, "The son of a bitch is bluffin', Hatch. Let's take 'em right here right now."

Boz smiled, took his hand away from the shotgun's forearm, and motioned to me. I jumped off the porch. Had my weapon in Hardy Tingwell's gut so quick he barely had time to blink.

"Here's how this is gonna work, fellers," Boz said.

"Everyone, 'cept Hatch and Hardy, will wheel his mount and head for the Matador, or get the hell out of town. Doesn't matter which to me. But if you're not gone by the time I count ten, Lucius and I will cut these two men in half. What happens after that won't mean much to anyone. Will it, John Roman?"

Hardy snorted, "Your reputation ain't worth a pile of horse dung around here, Tatum. Personally, I don't believe you've got the *huevos* necessary for an action that bold. Ain't no Ranger alive as audacious as you'd like us to believe."

Boz glanced across Hatch's saddle at the idiot Tingwell and said, "When it comes right down to the nut-cuttin', you stupid jackass, it's not really necessary for me to be all that *bold* anyway. See, I have a man in the cell block with your father. He's been told to shoot Bull if so much as one of you gets past us."

Over my shoulder, I shouted, "Rip, sing out. Got your shotgun on Bull?"

You'd of had to been deaf not to hear Thorn when he roared, "He's covered, boys. Quakin' in his boots. Figures he's about to meet his Maker, and he ain't far from wrong."

Rip's answer shocked Hardy Tingwell down to the soles of his well-used boots. Hatch and Longstreet shot nervous glances at each other. Both had strange puzzled looks on their faces.

Hatch touched Hardy's sleeve. Barely heard the gunman speak when he said, "Maybe this ain't such a good idea. Let's think on it a spell. Go over to the Matador. Have a drink and relax."

Boz didn't let a second pass when he snorted, "Thank God. Someone's finally showing something like a piece of brain today. Was beginning to wonder if any of you boys' thinker boxes worked."

Hatch, Longstreet, and Tingwell turned their animals and headed for the Matador. They kept glancing over their shoulders at us. For about a heartbeat, I felt certain ole Bull's hired killers might come back around and fight. But, I suppose, good sense must have got the best of them. Rest of the bunch followed like whipped dogs, and appeared disinclined to indulge murderous urges when it came to facing men like us.

Heard Boz let out a wheezing breath like a man who'd been hit in the gut. Knew he was relieved. Hell, my knees wobbled like a newborn calf's. Ocean of sweat saturated everything I wore. Propped the shotgun against my leg, and wiped my drenched hat out.

I said, "You know, Boz, we should have arrested Hardy for shooting Rip."

"We've got enough problems right now, Lucius. If we had jerked him up short, there'd of been a bloodbath for certain."

Stonehill whispered, "Damnation, boys. This has been the most tension-filled morning of my entire life. Lucky we ain't all three deader'n beaver hats."

Boz mumbled, "Yeah," turned on his heel, and headed for the jail.

Soon as we got inside, Rip threw the bolt on the heavy cell block door and jerked it open. He leaned against the frame and said, "Hell's bells, fellers. Gettin' mighty tense around these parts. Couldn't hear everything said back here in my hole, but got enough to know that about one more confrontation like that'n, and hot lead's gonna be flyin' like raindrops in a cyclone."

As he stood his weapon in the gun rack, Stonehill shook his head and said, "True enough. Neither Romulus Pitt nor Hardy Tingwell will go so easy next time." He turned to Boz. "You caught all of 'em by surprise with your audacity and bluster, Tatum. Such shenanigans won't work again."

"Hell of a mess," I said. "Town folk want us to let the old bastard go, Pitt wants to hang him. What's left of the Tingwell clan seems determined to break him loose first chance they get, and maybe kill some of us in the process. Prospects don't look good, any way you cut them."

Not sure Boz had put it all together quite so concisely up to that point. Or maybe Rip and I were just the first to string all the negatives of our situation together and say them out loud. Anyway, things got mighty quiet in Stonehill's office for a spell.

Boz mumbled, "On top of all that, both clans are in town drinking up every drop of bonded spider-killer they can get their grubby paws on. In about two hours they'll probably be out in the street drunk as skunks, and looking for a fight. God help us all if such an event comes to pass."

Let my mind go slipping around in the calm after the storm. Went so far as telling myself that the state of affairs couldn't get much worse. But, like my daddy always used to say, just when you think any given situation can't get any worse, it usually does. I swear, the man should've worked with a traveling circus as one of those crystal-ball gazers who claim to see the future.

Door burst open and slammed against the wall. Knob had slipped from Doc Adamson's sweaty hand. Poor man had all the outer appearance of someone on the verge of tears. He glanced at me, and then down at the floor. His arms hung at his sides as if broken at the shoulders. He shrugged and made a motion of tired resignation.

"Gentlemen, hate to be the bearer of bad news, but Miss Ruby Black just passed," he said.

16

"TOOK ONE THROUGH THE FRONT OF HIS SKULL"

MY CONFUSED MIND circled around the god-awful truth of his horrible report. The ghastly news slipped into my brain like one of the doc's scalpels slicing through soft flesh, but the words didn't make any sense. They carved across something at the back of my brain with such deadly effectiveness, my head snapped forward. Stars flew around the office in front of my unbelieving eyes.

Adamson's clinical pronouncement that she'd "just passed" took all the starch right out of me. My already wobbly legs went to rubber at the knees. Felt sure I was about to hit the ground like a felled tree.

Stumbled across the room, dropped into a chair, and thought I just might toss my breakfast all over the floor. I could hear people talking around me, but their remarks sounded as though everyone spoke from the bottom of a freshly filled rain barrel.

First thing that finally penetrated my brain was Adamson

saying, "Don't know for sure, Ranger. It seemed to me as though she just gave up." The doc's voice cracked as he ran a trembling hand through drenched hair and added, "Guess, maybe, she might have had an infection that festered and turned inside. Showed no evidence I could detect. Could be her heart simply gave out, what with all the different pieces of surgery necessary to repair the damage. Might've lost too much blood. Just don't know for sure."

Boz raised a hand to stop what sounded like the beginnings of a lengthy recitation of all the possible reasons for the dead girl's unfortunate departure from this earth.

My fevered mind swirled and heaved. The relationship with Ruby grew so quickly, burned with so much heat, and now ended so abruptly, I just couldn't get my wits around it.

Turned to Adamson and said, "But I saw her this morning. You said she'd be fine."

Man looked stricken. Even in my agitated state, I could tell he felt almost as lost as I did. He made a kind of beseeching motion with his hands and muttered, "I know, Lucius. Honestly, son, I had no reason to believe otherwise. I cannot, for the life of me, understand what went wrong. She simply stopped breathing. Tried my damnedest to bring her back. Nothing worked. I'm mystified by the turn of events."

Boz's spurs chinked and rang as he ambled over to my side. Jingling music from his silver rowels seemed out of place, given the circumstances and my precarious state of mind. He placed a sympathetic hand on my shoulder. Took every fiber of my being to keep from bursting into tears in front of men I respected.

My friend bent close to my ear and whispered, "Sometimes even witches make mistakes, son. Maybe Ruby wasn't your morning star."

Adamson had gone to mumbling. "Didn't think it went that deep. Yes, it was bad. But I've seen worse—lots of times.

Augie Smoot took one through the front of his skull—side to side, straight shot. Man's still alive. Has grandchildren. Course he does act mighty strange." He slumped into the only empty chair, cupped his head in his hands, and moaned, "Did my best, but sometimes people just die, Lucius. No understanding it when God decides to take them home with him."

That's when the rage boiled up again. Sprang from my chair, pistol in hand, and managed to get inside the cell block before anyone could stop me. Fired the first shot soon as I stepped over the threshold. Bullet ricocheted off a cell bar right in front of Bull Tingwell's face.

Prisoner went to screaming, scrambled for the farthest corner, and crawled under his cot like a turpentined cat. Snapped off another round that splintered a spot in the floor next to Tingwell's head, before Rip snatched my arm into the air and Boz grabbed me from behind. Gun went off again. Punched a nice-sized hole in the ceiling.

Boz yelled, "No, Lucius, no. Can't kill the woman-murderin' scum like this. I know you want to, but you can't."

Rip's grasp on my arm felt like iron bands tightening. After a spell of silent struggling, the blood to my hand stopped circulating. The pistol dropped from my grasp and bounced off the plank floor.

My frustration left me with nothing to do but scream at the old bastard. "God damn you and your whole worthless clan." Made a lunge for the cell door. Rip held me back. Screamed, "Another second alone and I'd of killed you deader'n a rotten tree stump, old man."

Rip held on and whispered, "Calm down now, Lucius. Don't want to hurt you. Calm down, son."

Crazy. Only way to explain it. Went completely crazy. First time it'd ever happened to me. Suddenly realized how such feelings might possess men. Cause a sensible fellow to do stupid, unreasonable things that land them at the end of a hangman's noose.

Anger, deeper than the blackest hole in Hell itself, finally drained out of me and, almost, seemed to seep through the cracks in the floor. Said, "I'm okay now, boys. You can let me go."

Snatched up my pistol from the corner, then headed for the jail's front door. I passed men on the street. Thought about killing both sides of Iron Bluff's set of belligerent jackasses, just for the sheer hell of it, but didn't. Had to make it to Ruby. Ran till I burst through Adamson's door. Stood beside what Ruby's spirit had left behind.

Fell on my knees next to her bed and wept. Sobs, too deep for a grown man to stand, racked my body like someone beating me in the back with a singletree from a Butterfield stagecoach. Ran a fevered hand over her cold, dead face and slid my fingers through her hair like a comb.

Leaned over and placed my head against her arm. Despite the odors of dried blood, carbolic, other antiseptics, and death, I could still smell the sweetness of her. She favored a toilet water that gave off the slightest hint of the fragrance from roses. To this very moment, every spring, the smell of roses has the power to transport me back to Ruby's side—and the edge of bitter tears.

"Why'd you have to leave?" I whispered into an unhearing ear. "We had wonders ahead of us, darlin'. So many years to share. Children to bring into this world. They'd have been beautiful, and smart, like their mother. You were supposed to grow old with me, Ruby."

I prayed to Adamson's tin ceiling. Questioned God's poor judgment in the matter and, finally, had to give her up. In those days people died. At times they went out singly, in pairs, even in large groups. Children passed in such numbers funerals for them were fairly commonplace—a daily occurrence. Disease, horrific accidents, or murder took them, right and left. Some killed one another for no good reason. I knew all those things to be true. Such knowledge didn't help me with her departure. Not even the least bit.

After an hour's worth of praying over unanswerable questions, from the deepest recesses of my wounded heart, I came to the startling realization that what passed for love between the two of us could well have been little more than misunderstood passion.

My status as the hero who'd saved her drew Ruby to me in a way that might never have survived the test of time. Hell, such a prospect could very well have been the way of future events. But, by God, Bull Tingwell had no right to keep us from the joy, or heartache, of discovering the error of our ways. The son of a bitch had stolen the future from us. I promised God he'd never again have another opportunity to commit such a heinous act.

Eventually Boz, Rip, and Doc Adamson came in and pulled me away from Ruby's lifeless body. They dragged me back to the jail. The walk helped, and by the time we arrived, I could think of little else but how Bull Tingwell would die.

In one of the blacker corners of my heart, I made plans for the old bastard's journey to his place in a festering Hell. Knew I might swing for his death; at that point, I didn't give a hoot in hell what befell me.

Perhaps the state of a troubled mind explains my reckless behavior a few hours later. My friends still hovered over me like two old-maid aunts. The Tingwell-Pitt situation had seemed to have calmed a mite when the jailhouse door popped open and a Pitt cowboy named Rusty Woolner hopped inside. The nervous Nellie danced from foot to foot like he had snakes in his drawers.

Boz said, "Well, what is it, boy? Spit it out."

Woolner held his hat by the brim and said, "Y'all best come on outside. Figure they's 'bout to be some killing done yonder in the street. Casper Longstreet done got Nick Fox hemmed up against the wall on t'other side of the Fin and Feather. Says he's gonna kill Fox and anyone else what gets in his way."

The words had barely tumbled from Wolner's lips when events beyond our control snapped everyone's head toward the door. Three pistol shots—one right after the other—shook the jail and rattled our windows. Sounded as though the shooter had thumbed them off as fast as humanly possible. Could barely detect a breath of silence between each blast.

All consideration of Bull Tingwell's unforgivable sin vanished. The four of us hit the door at a run. We grabbed shotguns on our way out. Remember thinking, this god-awful mess'll never end. Wondered how many more would have to die before God's vengeful wrath was satisfied.

Then a thought hit me like lightning from a clear blue sky. If things went badly in the next few minutes, I just might meet Ruby again on the other side. All it would take amounted to a single mistake.

With an overabundance of killers skulking around town, shaking hands with eternity was a fair likelihood. Just outside the jailhouse door, the acrid smell of spent gunpowder hit my nostrils. Very real prospect of cruel death came down hard.

Heard Boz say, "Keep your wits about you, boys. Don't want any of us dyin' today."

17

"HE'S DEAD AS JULIUS CAESAR"

SPOTTED CASPER LONGSTREET as soon as we rounded the corner of the Fin and Feather. He stood rooted to the ground in the middle of the street. Man appeared slightly humped over like he had a putrid stomach.

Cowboys and hired killers, from both clans, crowded the boardwalks in front of their chosen saloons. I passed through a swirl of drifting gunsmoke as we hoofed it in Casper's direction.

Like angry red wasps, me, Boz, Rip, and Stonehill fogged to within ten feet of Tingwell's ashen-faced gunfighter. Rip covered Pitt and his bunch. Boz and Stonehill took a bead on the Tingwell clan. I brought my weapon up on Longstreet. I was just before sending him to Kingdom, and final judgment, when he turned my way like a man under six feet of water.

A wine-colored, sticky-looking stain covered the hand clutched against his chest, and spread from the man's upper left side to the cartridge belt strapped high on his narrow waist. He took a single step my direction, stumbled, and almost fell. Cocked pistol dropped from his right hand and landed in the dusty street.

Bright bubble-filled blood oozed from the corner of his quivering mouth. Sounded bone-tired when he stammered, "J-just be damned. Nick Fox was b-better'n I thought." He glanced down at the holes in his chest and said, "Shit. B-bastard ruined my brannew shirt." Looked back up as though totally confused by the stunning turn of events, then dropped slap on his face like a head-shot steer. Once down, he didn't so much as twitch.

I knelt beside the man. Even when enjoying the best of health, Longstreet resembled one of those who'd already shaken Satan's scale-covered hand. Rolled the gunfighter over, and pressed a finger against his pockmarked neck. Nothing. It'd taken a lot of years, and a boatload of dead folk at Casper Longstreet's own hand, but he'd finally got his just deserts.

Threw a quick glance over at Boz and said, "He's dead as Julius Caesar." Quickly stood and swung my shotgun around on Pitt's crew.

Longstreet's bunch of loutish friends were rooted to the Matador's entrance by our show of force. Didn't stop them from yelling all manner of the bluest kinds of curses. Entire Tingwell crew realized their man was about to wake up shoveling coal in the furnaces of a sulfurous hell. That shattering insight didn't sit well with any of them.

Not to be outdone, Romulus led the Pitt gang in an equally rousing, and even more aggressive, response. Their hotly delivered blaspheming laced the air with the lewdest, most confrontational language an itinerant hard-shell Baptist evangelist could have imagined.

The disagreement escalated noticeably after about fifteen

seconds of such vigorous profanity. With itchy fingers wrapped around their pistol grips, men jumped from the boardwalks on both sides of the street. Death-dealing threats were shouted back and forth.

Whole scene settled a bit when I boldly stepped to within a few feet of where Nick Fox stood. He insolently leaned against the board fence that hid an empty lot between the Fin and Feather and the only barbershop in town. Bold son of a bitch had rolled, and lit, a cigarette during all the yelling. Smoke curled around his head like a shroud. I leveled my shotgun on his guts and cocked both barrels.

Didn't take long for everyone in attendance at that particular prayer meeting to realize another killing just might be in the offing. Leaders of both belligerent camps waved their angry men into silence. Of a sudden, the entire scene got so quiet a bald man could have heard the only hair left on his head grow. You would have needed a South Texas peon's razor-sharp machete to cut through the tension.

Fox had propped himself against the fence about twenty feet down the boardwalk from the Fin and Feather's batwing doors. Both the killer's holstered pistols still leaked pale wisps of blue-gray smoke. He held his hands out, palms facing me like a man pushing a door open. His eyes went dead. I could detect no sense of fear or remorse.

Fox said, "Tried to talk Casper out of this dance, Ranger Dodge. I harbored no desire to fight the man, given his deadly reputation and all. But, as you well know, comes a time when some folks wake up one morning and just seem determined to die." He waved at the crowds gathered in front of each saloon. "You can ask anyone on either side of the street. Casper goaded me into this shooting match. I even let him draw first."

Behind me I heard Boz call out, "That the way of it,

Hardy? Did your hired gun bring this death down on his own head?"

I turned slightly. Watched Hardy from the corner of my eye as he flicked a cigarette butt into the street and said to Boz, "Can't rightly say, Tatum. I wasn't in attendance when the disagreement started. Was inside the Matador havin' myself a whiskey repast. Why don't you look to someone else? Maybe one of these townsfolk seen it."

Crowd of locals had gathered on the street off to my left. Horace Breedlove stepped out of the swarm. Took a lot of gritty sand for what the man did next.

He kind of danced from foot to foot, tied and retied his apron four or five times, while rivers of sweat ran down his cheeks. Finally he said, "I seen it just the way Fox described, Ranger Tatum. Hell, everyone here seen this killing. Including you, Hardy. Ain't no reason to lie 'bout it now."

Can't say for sure, but I think it was John Roman Hatch who yelled, "Best keep your yap shut, you tater-dealin' son of a bitch."

Surprised me when the mild-mannered shopkeeper bulled up and shouted back, "I won't, by God." He gestured at the gathering of townspeople that milled about in a nervous knot behind him. "The *good* folk of Iron Bluff have had all we're willing to put up with from you two packs of murderous skunks. It's way past time for all you belligerent bastards to get your comeuppance. Sure wouldn't hurt any of our feelings if the whole damned lot of you ended up just like Longstreet."

Beat all I'd ever seen. Remember thinking, by God, the man's nervier than I would have ever given him credit for being. Course, near as I've been able to determine over the years, you never know just how far you can push men like Breedlove before they bite back.

The well-liked merchant's speechifying seemed to take

substantial fight out of Hardy Tingwell and his boys. Then Pruitt Pitt, who'd been quiet up to that point and should have kept his stupid mouth shut, popped off with the worst possible thing he could have said.

Boy stood behind his father and pointed at Hardy when he shouted, "And we stand ready to send all you living Tingwells to Hell on an outhouse door right here and now." Romulus Pitt turned as if to quiet his smart-aleck son, but never got the chance to say a single word.

Don't exactly know where the first shot came from. Way I stood in the street made it hard to see most of them boys. But it sounded like someone from the Pitt bunch fired the round that tipped us all into a bloody inferno. Could have been someone from either camp, though, I suppose.

Truth is, simply doesn't matter in the end. Felt like the concussion from that first blast almost blew my hat off. Marshal Stonehill went down like a burlap bag of horseshoes. Every hair on the back of my neck turned into barbed wire.

Nick Fox went for his guns. We were so close to one another the highly concentrated wad of a double fistful of lead damn near blew him in half. Dropped both hammers of the shotgun on his sorry ass. Splattered him all over the board fence. Pistols popped out of holsters all over the street like rabbits from a traveling magician's hat.

I headed for the doorway of the barbershop fast as I could hoof it. Arrived just in time to turn and watch as men from the Tingwell gang pushed their way into the Matador while wildly firing over their shoulders. Front window of that cow-country oasis exploded in a hailstorm of shattered glass.

Somehow Boz and Rip had managed to match me step for step, plus some, and crashed against the door as they fell beside me. We scrunched against the half-wood, half-glass door as tight as we could. Truth was, though, it didn't offer much in the way of shelter.

Turned to my right and said, "Either of you boys hit?"

Boz patted around on himself like a man looking for a smoke. "Not me. Leastways I can't find any extra holes right now."

Rip shook his head, but I noticed blood on the side of his head. I yelled, "Look to your ear, Rip. Think someone notched you up on top."

He fingered the gash and yelped, "I'll just be goddamned. Shot me again. Bet it was that sorry-assed Hardy Tingwell. Hell, I'm just now gettin' over the last time the evil bastard plugged me."

Boz snugged up against my back, tight as he could. Together we tried to peek around the door frame at the entrance of the Fin and Feather. Shattered glass, wood splinters, and dirt clods flew in every direction on both sides of the street. Horses screamed, and ran in all directions. One, still tied to the hitch rail, squealed and flopped sideways. Ran in place and tried several times to stand, but couldn't.

Boz leaned back against the barbershop door. "What'd you boys see?" Rip asked.

I said, "Not much. But I can tell you, without fear of contradiction, it does appear as though Stonehill has about as much pulse as a pitchfork." Intensity of the shouting, shooting, cussing, and general turmoil from both sides of the street made it almost impossible for me to hear either of my friends.

At first, all three of us thought we'd found a position of relative safety. Such dreamy notions only lasted until someone in the Matador spotted us. Bullets peppered the entry, front window, and plank boards of the walkway all around our hidey-hole. Hot lead blasted holes in the door frame, wall, and the barber's glass window.

Boz grabbed the shop's shiny brass knob and twisted. Entrance popped open. We fell across the threshold, and

scrambled inside to a higher degree of safety behind the
building's facade.

Rip lay down, rolled on his back, and kicked the door
shut. Leonard Skaggs, feller who owned Iron Bluff's only
tonsorial parlor, cowered behind his leather-covered chair.
Boz spoke to him, but the man shook all over and appeared
unable to reply.

Rip squirmed and wiggled himself toward the front glass
for a view outside. He yelled, "God Almighty. Sounds like
full-blown warfare out there. What we gonna do, Boz?"

My friend didn't reply. Before Thorn had a chance to
look outside, Boz motioned us toward the shop's back
door. We crawfished that direction. Rip grabbed Skaggs
and pulled him along. Got outside. Cover was much better
behind the flimsy building. Bullets had to go through at
least four walls to get to us instead of one.

Original builder had put up a six-foot-tall board-and-
batten fence that was as wide as Skaggs's hair-cutting operation and twelve to fourteen feet deep. We headed for the
corner on the south side, next to Romulus Pitt's Fin and
Feather saloon, and flopped down against the barbershop's
back wall. Everyone let out a sigh of relief, then sucked air
for a spell to try and calm down a bit.

Boz said, "Well, I knew when the final brawl came it'd
be bad. But hell, boys, no better'n most of these jackasses
can shoot, maybe we can keep the number of graves folks
around here have to dig to a minimum."

Rip shook his head. "Don't know about that 'un, Boz.
Put as much lead in the air as we've got flyin' around right
now, and any yahoo pullin' a trigger don't have to be much
of a shot to hit something."

I couldn't help but laugh. Surprised my friends. "What
the hell's so funny, Lucius?" Boz asked.

Shook my head and said, "Well, just think about it. Only

thing these idiots have killed so far, even with all this gunfire, is a town marshal owned by the Pitts that none of us
really trusted, and a horse. Not much to show for a fire-
works display that rivals the one they do over in Dallas
every Fourth of July."

A few seconds of silence passed between us as the thunderous blasting from the Fin and Feather grew more intense. Mr. Skaggs sat on his back entry stoop and covered
both ears with quaking hands.

Boz yelled, "Load 'em up. We've got to do something to
stop this, or we might well end up with a massacre on our
hands."

"What do you propose we do, Boz?" I asked.

Rip shouted, "Maybe we should just wait 'em out. They
can't keep up a barrage like this forever. Most of these
cowboys ain't carryin' a tubful of ammunition around with
'em."

"That might well be true," Boz shouted. "Then again, if
we don't take some kind of action, a lot more people could
end up dead."

"I'm game, Boz. What's the plan?" I asked.

He stood, and peeked over the fence, then quickly sat
back down. "There's a back door to the Fin and Feather not
thirty feet from where we're sittin'. Think what we'll have
to do is sneak in, throw down on the Pitt crew, and force
them to give up their guns."

Sounded good. Rip and I nodded as Boz rubbed his ear
and tried to figure out the rest of his plot. After about a
minute of scratching and thinking, he said, "Once we've
got 'em unarmed, we'll herd the whole bunch into this
fenced spot. Rip, you can guard 'em, while me and Lucius
see what we can do with all them boys over in the Matador."

Before we had an opportunity to respond, Boz jumped
to his feet and went to kicking at the fence. Took him a

right smart effort to make a hole. The planks didn't appear
to have been in place for very long. Green timber held to
the nails so tight, he really had to apply some force to
knock enough boards loose to allow a man Rip's size to get
through.

We rushed the Fin and Feather's back door, and stopped
long enough to make sure our shotguns were primed. Boz
said, "Lucius, go left. Rip, go right. Once we get inside and
set up, I'll give the signal. Fire one barrel into the air.
Gonna have to hope all of Pitt's boys will be behind whatever offers some degree of protection and facing the street.
Our entrance should surprise 'em some."

Rip and I nodded. Boz got his leg cocked to kick hell
out of the door. Rip reached down and turned the knob.
Heavy entrance swung open like it'd been waiting for our
arrival.

Boz stormed though first. Rip went in next. I brought up
the rear. Found ourselves in a poorly lit storage section
about twelve feet deep. Space occupied the entire back por-
tion of the saloon. About a third of the area was an office.
We peeked inside, but everyone appeared to be out front
showering the Matador with lead.

A batwing door separated the storage room and office
from the saloon's main hall. Noise level inside the building
was damned near deafening. Pitt's shooters couldn't have
heard us if we had chopped our way through the back door
with double-bit axes.

I stepped to the front of our parade and rushed past the
batwing. Stopped at the end of the Fin and Feather's beau-
tifully polished mahogany bar and waited for my friends.
Once we got lined up, Boz gave the signal. The three of us
cut loose at the same time.

Shattered ceiling matter rained down on everyone for a
dozen feet in front of us. Place got so quiet you could have

heard a pin drop on a cotton boll. You'd a thought a funeral was in progress.

Whining bullets from across the street still buzzed the air like angry bees as Boz yelled, "Throw down your weapons—or die this instant."

Men closest to us dropped their pistols—right damned quick. Those farthest away looked confused behind their overturned tables, chairs, and gaming fixtures.

One stupid jackass near the center of the room pointed his pistol at Rip. Thorn swung around and blew a double-fist-sized chunk of the poker table, near the man's head, to smithereens. Two or three pieces of shot caught the poor goober in the cheek. He went to rolling around on the floor. Screamed like a little girl.

Rip's decisive action got the attention of everyone there. Pistols hit the floor like raindrops.

Boz swung his shotgun around from man to man and roared, "Any more such treachery, and we'll kill the son of a bitch who tries it."

Rip was so mad he made them jaybirds crawl outside. Whole bunch of them had their lips stuck out like buggy seats. All told, we hustled Pitt, his sons, and eight others into the fenced spot behind Leonard Skaggs's barbershop. Rip blocked the opening we'd kicked in the fence.

As Boz and I headed out behind the Fin and Feather, for a spot on the far side of the jail, I heard Rip yell, "Any of you bastards move, and there won't be enough left of your sorry hide to tan and fashion into a coin purse."

Huffed and puffed our way to the south corner of Iron Bluff 's lockup. Gunfire from the Matador, which had been hotter than election day in a yellow jacket's nest, had dried up to nothing more than a random shot or two here and there.

We stepped from behind our cover, and were about to

slip across the jail's porch to the shelter afforded by the Fin and Feather's wall, when the sound of pounding and sawing inside the jail got our attention. Racket stopped us both dead in our tracks.

Boz whispered, "What the hell you suppose that is, Lucius?"

Cocked an ear that direction and said, "Sounds like someone hammering on a cell door. You reckon some of Bull's boys got inside and are trying to break him out?"

Boz broke his shotgun open, checked the loads, and snapped it shut. He flicked a finger at my weapon, and I did the same. "You ready to storm our own jail?" he asked.

Dropped a fresh round in a spent barrel of my blaster and said, "Don't see me sitting on my hands, do you? Lead the way, amigo."

We stepped onto the jail's tiny veranda as quietly as we could. Boz pushed the door open. John Roman Hatch stood beside the open entry to the cell block. Gunman had his back turned toward us. We took him totally by surprise.

Tingwell's most famous hired killer whirled our direction. Both his bone-handled pistols came up. Boz and I fired at the same time. God Almighty, but the spray of lead shot damn near blew him all to pieces, and painted the entire wall with gore.

Soon as Hatch hit the floor in a busted heap, all glassy-eyed and spitting up his guts, we fired our second volley through the open cell block door. Men screamed in pain and called on God for mercy. I heard the heavy thumps of bodies hitting the floor.

While a dense cloud of black powder smoke hung in the air, Boz and I slipped to either side of the open doorway, reloaded, and waited. Nothing else happened. No response. I'd figured on someone firing back.

I yelled, "Come on out. Do it now or die."

Right certain Hardy Tingwell was the one who yelled back, "Go to hell, Dodge, or come on in and get us." Bit of heated discussion from inside after his amazingly stupid pronouncement. On his fingers, Boz counted off at least three different voices. Didn't matter how many were inside anyway, because no one came out or offered to give up.

Put my hat over the muzzle of my shotgun and eased the decoy around the jamb. Pistol fire blew it across the room and almost back into the street. We crossed our big boomers over one another and fired both barrels into the cell block, without even aiming. Our X-shaped coverage sprayed the entire area with buckshot. By God, got real quiet then.

After about a minute of reloading and listening for any kind of movement, we stepped inside to an absolutely horrific scene. Hardy Tingwell and Icy Winters had managed to pry the cell door open enough to the point where Bull was stuck, half inside and half outside. Our blasting had peppered the hell out of the three of them.

Winters took most of what we sent their way. He was an ugly lump of buzzard bait. But Hardy and Bull managed to survive. Looked to me as though Hardy cowered behind Winters when he saw our weapons pop around the corner, pointed in their general direction. Bull, as is the case with old people in general, simply got lucky. He might have suffered a dozen or so minor pieces of shot in his ancient hide, but none of them did any permanent damage.

Boz found the keys and locked father and son in an undamaged cell. Then, we headed for the street again. Gunfire had completely ceased.

Boz said, "I'd bet all of Tingwell's cowboys have been left leaderless and can't figure out why the Pitt bunch ain't firing back."

"You're probably right, Boz. But how're we gonna get them to give up on this ruckus and come out of the Matador?"

"Oh, hell, that 'uns easy. Watch this," he said, then took about six steps into the street.

"Damnation, Boz," I hissed.

He stopped and yelled, "You boys in the Matador, listen up. Icy Waters is dead. John Roman Hatch is dead. Casper Longstreet is dead. Your employers are behind bars. After some persuasion from the Texas Rangers, Pitt and his crew gave up and are under our guns at this very moment. It's way past time to put your weapons aside, fellers. This dance is over."

Didn't take them long to come to a decision. Seven men filed out of the Matador, hands raised and looking like whipped dogs.

Boz strolled over and gave Tingwell's boys a hot-mouthed lecture about how their lives were precious and how the whole damned bunch was right before pissing them away for an old man not worth the mud on their boots. He told them they should saddle up, turn their faces west, and get the hell out of Iron Bluff as quick as they could. I sincerely believe most of them took his advice.

Few minutes after his first lecture, Boz hit Pitt and his bunch with pretty much the same harangue. Not sure his speech had the desired effect. Only about half of them lit out when given the chance. Thank God Alvin Clements decided to go with them. That only left Romulus and his idiot sons. We locked them up right next to Bull and Hardy Tingwell. Lot of angry mouthing between the clans for a day or so.

Took a spell to bury all the dead folk and get those with wounds tended. Hell, I didn't care about anyone but Ruby. Boz and me found her a nice plot in the town cemetery on a bluff that overlooked the Angelina. Reminded me some of where Bull buried his daughter.

After her hastily arranged funeral, which almost every decent citizen in town attended, Mr. Pinkus pulled me aside and said, "I've something you might be interested in."

He led me to the back of his mortuary, then outside to a rough shed. In one corner stood a piece of statuary covered with dusty canvas. With a bit of overly dramatic flare, he snatched the rough covering away. Beneath, a marble angel kneeled and gazed lovingly toward heaven. A single huge tear trickled down its cheek. I damn near collapsed right on the spot.

Pinkus said, "Used to have a feller named Osgood Stange living in these parts. Owned most of the land the Tingwells bought. Osgood sent for this piece to place on his daughter's last resting place. Girl died of pneumonia at the age of eight. Sad death. Unfortunately, her angel didn't arrive until about a week after Osgood passed on himself. He hadn't paid me, so she's been sitting here under this piece of canvas for nigh on five years."

Finally regained my composure and said, "Put it at the head of Miss Black's grave. Carve her name on the base. Don't know the right dates, but I'll send them to you once we get back to Fort Worth." Started to walk away, stopped, and said, "Also, below the name carve, 'Her family's morning star.'"

Pinkus gave me a feeble smile and said, "I knew you'd like it. Don't you want to know the price, Ranger Dodge?"

As I turned and walked away, I said, "No. The money doesn't matter. Just do it."

Boz kept our prisoners locked up for almost two weeks. One night after supper, we were sitting outside on the porch when he said, "Well, Lucius, I had hoped Judge Cooper would have made town by now. Can't keep these men locked up much longer. All the killings they're connected to seem mutual 'cept Ruby's. Been thinkin' 'bout settin' all of 'em loose, except Bull."

"Even Hardy? Hell, he shot Rip and tried to kill me."

"I know, but you got him back pretty good. Doc Adamson spent almost four hours pickin' out all the lead we put in his sorry ass. Boy might not ever walk again. Figure you punished him for his sins. Don't you?"

"Yeah, I suppose." Leaned my chair against the wall and said, "Then what?"

He thought my question over, then said, "Think I'll have Rip take Bull to the law over in Shelbyville. That way Judge Cooper should be able to get him before the court for trial a lot quicker. But you know, could be possible Bull might try to escape on the way. Rip may even have to kill the old bastard. I think such a prospect is pretty much a certainty. What do you think, Lucius?"

"Long as he's dead, I don't give a hoot in Hell how it happens."

Boz smiled. "Good. I'll put Rip on the road tomorrow. We won't tell anyone. Should give him plenty of time to get as far away as he can, before anyone finds out Bull's done went and bit the dirt. We'll turn the rest of 'em out a day or so later. Then, we can head for Fort Worth. How's that sound?"

Well, by God, it sounded just fine. Worked out exactly the way Boz planned too. Heard later, when news of Bull Tingwell's unfortunate departure from this earth got back to Iron Bluff, the remaining members of his family packed up and disappeared like thieves in the night. Most folks around town considered their departure good riddance. The Pitt clan threw a family get-together. Danced till the sun came up.

Six months later, Romulus bought all the property the Tingwells vacated for about a nickel on the dollar. Few weeks after getting what he'd always wanted, the elder Pitt

went out for a ride. On his way past the former Tingwell
manor house, a pack of wild dogs attacked him, brought
his horse down, and ripped the man to pieces. Least that's
the way the story got told.

Me and Boz headed back to Fort Worth. Did a swing
through Lone Pine and picked up Orvis Tate. He damn
near drove us both crazy before we turned him over to the
Tarrant County sheriff.

Worst morning of my young life was when we reported
the sad news about Ruby's unfortunate death to Captain
Culpepper. Only time in my memory I saw the cap'n openly
weep. We offered to accompany him when he delivered the
news to her family. He refused, and made the trip alone.

EPILOGUE

AN OVERABUNDANCE OF years have passed since what became widely known as the Tingwell-Pitt War. So many years, in fact, most folks completely forgot it ever happened. I suppose just about everyone connected with the event is dead now, with the exception of me.

Rangered for nigh on four decades, before I finally had to hang up my guns. Every other year or so, I'd make a special swing through East Texas. Stop for a visit at Ruby's final resting place. Funny thing. Graveyard suffered from serious neglect as time passed, but Ruby's was the only site where flowers flourished—and weeds never grew. Last time I went by, her weeping angel looked exactly the way it did the day Pinkus set the statue in place.

Used to occasionally receive a missive from Cloud Quigley's daughter. Old ink-slinger passed a few years after all the shouting, shooting, and dying. By then, Iron Bluff had pretty much fallen apart, dried up, and faded away. As

I understand, there's nothing left these days but windblown nothingness.

In one of her letters the Quigley girl, think her name was Lydia, told as how she found an unpublished story Cloud wrote about me, Boz, and the war. Said she remembered seeing me in Iron Bluff when she was but a nubbin. Thought I was the most dashing figure of a man who ever donned a palm-leaf sombrero and Mexican spurs. Must have been real easy to impress kids back then, I suppose. Couldn't rightly remember little Lydia, though. And we never did manage a meeting. I've wished a thousand times I could bring her to mind. She just ain't with me these days, if she ever was.

But every so often something, or someone, like that red-haired, blue-eyed beauty coming out of Cooley Churchpew's place, brings unexpectedly fond recollections of Ruby Black to the front of my rapidly fossilizing brain. And if the moon's right, and I can get my head situated on the pillow at just the perfect angle, dreams have the power to bring her to me for a brief visit.

My visions of Ruby are consistently the same. I'm stretched out on a blanket, laid in the grass along the banks of the Angelina. Blooming wildflowers fill the lazy breezes with fragrant perfume. A soft, cool hand caresses my brow. My mind fights to force contrary eyes open. Her lips touch mine. As she draws away, I wonder at such astonishing beauty. Unlike me, she's never aged. Forever twenty years old. And when I come fully awake, her touch lingers on my lips and the places where her hand rested on my arm are still warm.

One time I fell asleep in my favorite chair out on the back porch. I'd had a few dippers of fine sippin' whiskey that night. Well, maybe more than a few. Kind of snapped awake about three in the morning. Swear 'fore Jesus, Ruby stood over the chair. Could feel her fingers on the back of my neck.

Sweet girl smiled and said, "Won't be long now. We'll be together again, Lucius. I'm waiting."

Then, she vanished. Like I'd snapped my fingers and caused her to disappear. Strange, ain't it? I rarely give a second's worth of thought to the gunfights, death, or bad blood of Iron Bluff. But Ruby, oh, my friends, there's a whole different story. I admit to being quite unprepared for the mark she left on my heart. Surprise of my life, for while all else fades, she is forever with me.

Guess I'll hold up on my scribbling for a spell. Gonna stroll down to Cooley's. He's got a damned fine pool table in back of his place. Grab me an RC Cola from his icebox, drag up a cane-bottomed chair, and watch Sulphur River's young fellers shoot a game or two of nine ball. That fiery-haired little gal could stop in again, you know. I might even offer to buy her a bottle of pop. Damned fine way to spend an afternoon, don't you think?